Lying in state

'I will not be burying Mr Charles Beauregard under such flags and roses and the like,' said Father Flanagan fiercely. 'I said it to his face when he was alive and I'll not be holding my tongue when he's dead. I denounce the Red Rose and all its works. An insult to the dead, and to Almighty God and to his sorrowing family.'

'Are you referring to me, Father?' said a clear female voice from somewhere above their heads. Jemima realized for the first time that there was a gallery in the plain church. She looked back. The gallery, which ran the width of the church, over its doorway, was totally empty except for one girl, sitting in the centre on what looked remarkably like a kind of wooden throne.

'Since I am the only member of this family sorrowing over the death of Charles Beauregard, it is my request that the Red Rose is present,' continued the high clear voice. 'I instruct you, Father, to proceed with my brother's funeral.' She paused, and looked furiously, disdainfully, at the rest of the congregation below her. 'I regard the rest of you, as you well know, as murderers.'

'Her Majesty Queen Clementina,' murmured Captain Lachlan with something like reverence. He even managed a kind of bow.

'Murderers,' repeated Miss Clementine Beauregard.

The
WILD
ISLAND

Antonia
FRASER

BANTAM BOOKS
New York • Toronto • London • Sydney • Auckland

THE WILD ISLAND

A Bantam Crime Line Book / published by arrangement with
W. W. Norton & Company, Inc.

PRINTING HISTORY

Norton edition published 1978
Bantam edition / September 1991

CRIME LINE and the portrayal of a boxed "cl"
are trademarks of Bantam Books, a division of
Bantam Doubleday Dell Publishing Group, Inc.

ISBN 0-553-29324-9

Published simultaneously in the United States and Canada

Printed in the United States of America

OPM   0 9 8 7 6 5 4 3 2 1

For Benjie and all at Eilean Aigas

Bonnie Prince Charlie ∽ Marjorie Stuart of Eilean Fas

Charlotte Clementina Stuart m. Robert Beauregard of Kilbronnack
b. 1746

(Beauregards of Kilbronnack)

Colonel Henry m. Lady Edith de Bourne
(Henry Benedict
Beauregard)

Ben   Rory   Hamish   Gavin   Niall   Kim
b. 1940   b. 1942   b. 1943   b. 1945   b. 1946   b. 1960

Colonel Carlo   m   Leonie Fielding Ney
(Charles Edward   d. 1955
Beauregard)
killed 1944

Charles   Clementina
b. 1945   b. 1945

The Beauregards of Castle Beauregard

CONTENTS

ONE

A Highland Welcome

As Jemima Shore arrived at Inverness Station, it was early morning but already the sun was shining. She thought: I'm arriving in Paradise. At that moment a man's voice said in her ear:

'All this way for a funeral.' It was an intimate voice. Almost purring. Jemima felt uncomfortably startled. She looked round.

Behind her a man of a certain age, tall, cadaverous, was bending down to pick up a suitcase. A younger man of much the same ilk was standing beside him. Possibly they were related. Both were dressed with extreme formality for the place—a station—and the time—it was 8.30 am. Jemima had just emerged from her sleeper. She did not feel up to such a situation, at least until she had had a cup of coffee. Whichever of the two men had spoken, it was nothing to do with her. She turned her head back and concentrated on the prospect of a porter.

'It's not all that bad, Colonel Henry,' said a second voice. 'In fact, in some ways it's good. In some ways it's very good indeed.'

Jemima shivered. She was glad she did not know, and never would know, anything more about a funeral to which it was possible to have anything but unmixed reactions of sorrow. She stepped firmly onto the platform. She had come here to get away from that sort of thing. The first sight which met her eyes was an enormous splashed scarlet graffiti on a hoarding opposite.

'Up the Red Rose!' it screamed and then something beneath in what looked like Gaelic, as well as an old separate sort of calligraph, which she couldn't make out at all. The scarlet letters were imposed wilfully on another, more formally written, white notice. To her irritation, she found herself trying to make it out instead of concentrating on the task of finding a porter, or even a barrow. Stronger men than her, with dogs and gun cases to reinforce their claim, were apparently engaging all conceivable porterage. 'A Highland Welcome,' the original notice had read. That at least was friendly.

Of course the inhabitants of the Highlands could still welcome Jemima weekly on their television sets, if they were so minded. As 'Jemima Shore, Investigator' in a series put out by Megalith Television under that title, she generally found her way into the ratings. Jemima's speciality was in fact serious-minded sociological enquiry—housing, deprived families, these were the kind of topics which interested her; but the title of the series played on the notion of an amateur detective. That title had been an early inspiration of her boss, Cy Fredericks. Sometimes she felt that it had become almost too memorable, too much of a catch-phrase for journalists and cartoonists alike. But MTV, entranced by the series' prolonged success, would not dream of changing it.

Before her departure she had recorded what seemed like a monumental number of programmes in her new series. The public would switch on. But she herself would be absent—in Paradise. The sun was still shining. In fact it had been shining all of the ten minutes since her arrival at Inverness Station and not a drop of rain in sight.

She needed a rest from curiosity. All the same, who were they welcoming? 'HRH,' those were the next letters, partly obscured by the word 'Red.' After that it was easy: 'A Highland Welcome to HRH Princess Sophie of Cumberland.' So Hurricane Sophie, as television had irreverently nicknamed the young Princess, was visiting the Highlands, was she?

That was yet another fact which need not concern Jemima Shore. Funerals, royal visits, none of that was going to stop her enjoying a well-deserved rest away from it all. And on an island. Could anything be further away from it all than a Scottish island in the middle of a fast-flowing river, complete with cliffs and chasms to protect its privacy?

Two men watched her alight. Unlike the funeral party, this second pair was dressed in such a nondescript fashion as to rouse exactly that suspicion which they presumably intended to avoid.

'Look, Miller, that's Jemima Shore,' said the more stolid-seeming of the two. 'I fancy her.' He made his approval sound like an announcement from the pulpit.

'She was on the box last night,' the man named Miller spoke wonderingly.

'She's always on the box.'

'But she's not always at Inverness Station. And come to think of it, Tyne, nor are we. Where's HRH then?'

'HRH is putting the finishing touches. Plenty of time.' The man named Tyne continued to look lugubriously after Jemima Shore, whose figure was vanishing down the platform. Her hair, its pure Madonna-like style made famous by television, ruffled slightly in the breeze. 'My wife fancies her too. She's somewhat the same type, my wife. Same colouring and hairstyle. Once in a shop, someone came up to her...'

A discreet cough interrupted these reminiscences, and as a glimpse of something bright and girlish, red, a coat, a hat, perhaps, was seen through the corridor window, both men proceeded to give their full attention to the interior of the train, rather than the outside world of the platform.

If Jemima Shore noticed the heads turning at all, it was in some automatic register of her brain. It meant absolutely nothing to her. The only sign of recognition she would welcome this morning would be from her future landlord Charles Beauregard. And he was to convey her, rapidly she hoped, away from the panoply of Inverness Station *en fête* to her much-desired Highland retreat.

But twenty minutes later, sitting in the Railway Hotel, whose name belied its distinct if old-fashioned grandeur, there was still no Charles Beauregard to rescue Jemima Shore. She was now surrounded by her luggage, one of the dog-and-guncase set having condescended to share a vast truck with her. But the effect of the multitude of suitcases distributed round her in the lounge of the hotel was to make her feel like someone who had been shipwrecked. It was expensive American luggage acquired during her last trip to the States and her enthusiastic young secretary Cherry had insisted on having it all stamped with her full name.

'Oh, Jem, you never know when it might help. Your name being so famous in every corner of the globe. In a tight corner, it might prove invaluable.' Cherry had a vivid if cliché-ridden imagination. To her, all corners were tight, and all names in television famous throughout the universe.

Now, Jemima reflected sardonically, here was a tight corner indeed. Herself sitting with her luggage in a remote corner of the world—surely the Highlands of Scotland qualified for that—with absolutely no way of getting to the holiday cottage she had rented for a month. No telephone. No directions. And an address which at the time had struck her as infinitely romantic, but now as rather ludicrously imprecise: 'Eilean Fas, Inverness-shire.'

The staff of the Railway Hotel was amiability itself. Part of this amiability extended to the fact that its members had no objection to her sitting there indefinitely; they neither pressured her into partaking of breakfast, or otherwise enquired of her intentions. But it was no good pretending that this mountain of luggage proclaiming the name of Jemima Shore was cutting any ice with them whatsoever.

Jemima took out Charles Beauregard's letter which was rapidly becoming her last link with her projected holiday. 'Beauregard Estate Office,' it was headed, 'Kilbronnack.'

Dear Miss Shore,

This is to confirm the arrangement made over the telephone with your secretary. You will rent the cottage known as Tigh Fas on Eilean Fas for one month starting from . . .

Yes, right day, right month. Not that Cherry could fail, but clearly Beauregard Estates could and in a sense had done so. The letter ended:

As Eilean Fas is difficult to find, and the bridge rather tricky, it seems simplest if I meet you in Inverness with the Land-Rover. I can explain details about the cottage, heating, etc, then and hand over the keys.

I should tell you that you won't be able to get television on Eilean Fas but if there is anything special you want to see you can always come over to the Castle to watch it.

I look forward to meeting you.

The letter itself was carefully typed, and the signature: Charles Edward Beauregard, careful—even measured—in the writing. But there was a scrawled PS, where the writing was larger and not so tidy. It gave the impression of being written under some stronger impulse than the mere details of a holiday let:

PS. There is another matter concerning Eilean Fas which I should like to talk to you about personally. It can't be put in a letter.

Jemima Shore, however, was not the slightest bit interested in the personal details of the island, nor for that matter how and when to watch television in the Highlands— perish the thought! She wanted a Land-Rover and breakfast, preferably in that order. In short she wanted a Highland Welcome, such as had been promised to Princess Sophie—or any welcome. But if not, at least breakfast.

Jemima made a decision. She went to the reception desk and said in her most pleasant, brisk manner: 'My name is Jemima Shore.'

The receptionist was quite a young girl with dark hair and healthy pink cheeks. Jemima did not pause for any possible reaction. 'And I am waiting here for Mr. Charles Beauregard. If he arrives and asks for me, will you tell him I am in the dining room having breakfast?'

But the girl behind the desk continued to stare at Jemima. Her mouth was truly open, a rare phenomenon. And she said nothing at all. Jemima wasn't even quite certain she had taken in the message. As for this fan reaction, it was all that Cherry could have hoped for. So she repeated:

'Mr. Charles Beauregard. You know Mr. Beauregard?' The letter had stated the arrangement clearly enough: 'We'll meet at the Railway Hotel, where they know me, and Alistair, the head porter, is an old friend of mine.'

The girl gave a strangled sound which could at least be interpreted as 'Aye,' and immediately dived through the little door at the back of the reception desk cubicle.

Jemima passed into the dining room where a series of vast pictures of steam trains rushing through Highland gorges enlivened the otherwise tomb-like room. There were a number of scattered breakfasters. Two of them, seated at a table near the door, were conspicuous in their dark suits. Jemima recognized them from the train and that snatch of rather eerie conversation. The rest wore tweeds, jeans, thick jerseys and even—on one very stout and elderly man—a kilt.

A huge dog was roaming about among the tables. A labrador? Or was it a St. Bernard? Its head came up nearly to the level of the table. Jemima was vague about dogs, the intricacies of their breeding and maintenance never having penetrated her world of television—and she herself never having led that kind of settled domestic life which would either inspire her or enable her to own one. Jemima felt an affinity for cats, cats headed by her own long-haired white-pawed tabby, with her mackerel markings, Colette.

This dog was beige, although that was probably the wrong word when applied to a dog. Jemima, however, admired the colour beige; it was in fact her favourite colour and she was wearing it at the moment. Beige, a great deal of it, including beige trousers, from a man's tailor (for free, as a discreet advertisement), beige silk shirt (Yves St. Laurent, in no way for free), beige and white pullover (ditto). Even the boots beneath the tailored trousers were dark beige.

The dog, she thought, would make an artistic addition to the ensemble. The dog seemed to think so too. He came snuffling up to the table where the waiter had installed her, wagging his tail as though he hoped to sweep the room with it, and disturbing many tablecloths around him as a result. He put his huge head in Jemima's lap and looked at her passionately.

'Jacko!' shouted the elder of the two men in the dark suits. Then with more fury: 'Jacobite.' His voice entirely lacked the purring note of that remark in the train. It had great authority, was even stentorian.

'Jacobite—here, boy.' The dog turned and bounded with instant obedience in the direction of his master. It was an impressive performance. Although Jemima could not easily imagine anyone, man or beast, or even woman, disobeying that voice.

Moodily, she ordered a breakfast of things Scottish, more because she thought she ought to, than because she was any longer very hungry: finnan haddock, which was delicious. The coffee was awful. She sipped it, wondering whether the next step was to ring up Cherry—a confession of failure considering how firmly she had announced: 'I'm away for a month, Cherry. No letters which aren't urgent, which means no letters. No calls—you can't telephone me anyway and I'm not going to trudge to a Scottish call box to call you. No telegrams if you can resist it.' Cherry loved telegrams, whose language satisfied the dramatic side of her nature. No, she really did not want to telephone Cherry just twelve hours after that conversation.

How maddening for the Estate Office not to give its telephone number on the writing paper. Kilbronnack itself must have telephones even if the islanders didn't.

At that point in her musings she was aware of the older man in the dark suit standing over her. For a moment, confused, she thought he had come to say something about the dog, since Jacobite had followed his master back across the room and was once more lifting his nose to the table, sniffing the elixir of the remains of Jemima's breakfast.

'Miss Shore?' he was saying. 'Good morning. I'm Henry Beauregard.'

Jemima's first reaction was enormous relief that at last a Beauregard—if not the right one, at least a member of the family—was taking an interest in her cause.

'Ailsa at the desk was telling me you were having some difficulty in getting to the funeral,' remarked this Beauregard. He really did have a most attractive voice when it was lowered. In fact, altogether Henry Beauregard was an attractive as well as a distinguished-looking man, with his bony face set off by thick hair, grey but showing streaks of what must have been the original black. Jemima thought of Hamlet's father, 'a sable silvered.' Although there was nothing particularly fatherly in the manner of Henry Beauregard. And his hair too was curiously long for a man who in other ways was so conventionally dressed. It added to the romanticism of his appearance.

However, Henry Beauregard, attractive as he might be, appeared to be under a slight misapprehension as to the reason for her presence in the Highlands.

'Oh, no,' said Jemima quickly. 'There's been a mistake. I was trying to leave a message for Charles Beauregard. Your brother or cousin or something? Anyway, he's coming to fetch me. I thought the girl didn't understand at the time.'

Henry Beauregard stared at her. For such a totally poised man he looked genuinely startled.

'I'm afraid there's no mistake, Miss Shore,' he said after a pause. 'And my nephew will hardly be coming to fetch you, I fear. You see, we are on our way to his funeral. Charles Beauregard is dead.'

TWO

Terribly Sudden

The first reaction of Jemima Shore, which she did not in fact express, was: 'Oh God, there goes my holiday...'

Instead she said in a tone of perfectly modulated regret: 'I'm sorry.' She added equally perfectly: 'Was it terribly sudden?'

Henry Beauregard continued to stare at her. Jemima felt her cool beginning to abandon her.

'I mean, I had a letter from him only the other day.' It was a ridiculous remark and the dog seemed to think so too. He looked at her with exceptional mournfulness and wandered away to another table, his tail wagging.

'You were—great friends?' Henry Beauregard was purring again. She recognized the note, both sinister and attractive.

'No, no, we'd never even met.' Charles Beauregard's uncle did not appear to know how to deal with this.

After a moment he said reverently, 'Charles was a very special person.'

'Oh, I know,' replied Jemima with equal reverence. Then she thought: This is ridiculous. I never knew him. I have absolutely no idea, no idea whatsoever, what he was like. I must step out of all this. Now.

'Was it terribly sudden?' she asked again. There was more authority, less reverence, in her voice. Henry Beauregard seemed to recognize it. He positively drew to attention.

'Oh God, yes, terribly sudden.' There was a pause while he seemed to be considering what to say next.

'Colonel Henry, we really must be going,' said a third voice, interrupting them. It was the younger man in the dark suit. The only person now absent from the party was Jacobite, currently sniffing at the feet of the elderly man in the kilt. Jemima regarded the younger man; no, he did not really have the appearance of being related to her interlocutor. Just a generic likeness in the handsome, slightly craggy features. It was the dark suit which had given them a certain funereal resemblance.

To begin with, this man was not only younger but shorter. And now she examined him, his black suit was fancy and ridiculous where Colonel Henry's was ancient but becoming, while his voice lacked both the seductive purr and the stentorian command of his companion's.

'Miss Shore,' said Colonel Beauregard. 'May I introduce our local MP, Ossian Lucas?'

Jemima Shore felt as surprised as if, with memories of Anglo-Saxon at Cambridge, she had met Beowulf's Grendel the Dragon. And failed to recognize him. Ossian Lucas!

The famed MP for the English Highlands, as *Time* Magazine would put it. And although Lucas had only occupied the seat since the October '74 election, *Time* Magazine had already found occasion to put it just like that. What with Scottish nationalism and Scottish inter-nationalism and Scottish devolution and Scottish revolution... The great thing about Scotland was that it was news these days. And Ossian Lucas was news too.

His clothes for one thing. On closer inspection Ossian Lucas's dark suit was waisted as though for Spanish dancing, unlike that of Colonel Henry which proceeded majestically from high neck to lower ankle without interruption as though according to some prearranged law. And was there not some hint of velvet, black but velvet all the same, on his collar and a suspicion of black frogging about the buttonholes?

Jemima, indeed, felt quite surprised that Ossian Lucas, MP, had been sitting in the Railway Hotel, Inverness, all that time without one newspaper reporter making an appearance. That must explain her failure to recognize him. Of course she had not seen a copy of this morning's *Highland Clarion*. That might well contain the headline OSSIAN LUCAS IN INVERNESS.

Ossian Lucas. Was he even Scots?

There were those, all too many of them, who would swear to having been at a minor English public school with one Oswald Lucas. The trouble with these mischief-makers was that they had all been at different schools.

Ossian Lucas, like the legendary Gaelic bard for whom he had presumably been named either by his parents or himself, might be suspected of being the product of a forgery. But it was mighty difficult to prove.

Anyway he was the MP for the Highlands and Islands constituency. On the whole, Jemima felt warmly towards MPs. Her former lover Tom Amyas was a former MP— losing his seat in the October '74 election. He now worked permanently for the vociferous Welfare Now Group, where rumour had it that he had become close to his youthful acolyte Emily Crispin. Jemima believed the rumour.

Jemima's own affair with Tom had ended with one passionate and prolonged—all night—row; this took place shortly after the strange events involving Jemima at the Convent of the Blessed Eleanor, Churne. In a way they had both turned to acolytes for consolation. Tom had sought out his aide at the WNG, the silent and devoted Emily; Jemima had turned to Guthrie Carlyle, handsome, rather more loquacious than Emily, a few years younger than herself, equally devoted and her producer on the 'Jemima Shore, Investigator' programme at Megalith Television.

But she remained on the side of MPs.

She was even prepared—cautiously—to be on the side of Ossian Lucas.

'Oh God,' cried Ossian Lucas, looking at her. 'The press! Why won't they leave one in peace?' He struck his temple with what Jemima expected to be one lily-white hand. On close inspection it was not white. Merely a hand pressed to a brow in a slightly extravagant gesture. Rather a muscular workmanlike hand. With a quick look at Colonel Henry, Jemima realized that he was the one with the long artistic white hands.

'I'm not the press any more than you are," retorted Jemima in an equally muscular tone, recalled to reality from fantasies of MPs and Scotland and long white hands. 'I'm here on holiday. Or rather I was intending to be here on holiday.' She gazed at Colonel Beauregard as beseechingly as she could.

'Colonel Beauregard,' she proceeded with a very passable fluttering eyelash, 'I was renting a cottage from your—er—nephew—we've never met—I mean we never had met—but he was going to meet me—' Oh, the English language. This was hopeless.

But Colonel Henry was already purring. There was no other word for it.

'A tenant!' He might have been saying: A Magician! A Martian! Or whatever your particular fancy was. There was such a mixture of delight and lust in his voice. 'I thought you were a *friend* of poor Charles.' Into the word friend, it had to be admitted, went a very different mixture of expressions. Contempt. Pity. Almost ridicule.

'A friend of Charles—Jemima Shore,' said Ossian Lucas. 'That's hardly likely.' There was the same ambiguity, an unpleasant irony, which she remembered from the remark in the train. How she wished, in view of all this unexpected intimacy, that she did not remember that sinister little exchange. She felt like someone who arrives to stay in an unknown house, blunders into an unlocked bathroom and finds subsequently that the invaded naked stranger is her host.

'What are we going to do about you?' Colonel Henry was purring again. Jacobite was back, sniffing. He seemed to emphasize the affectionate, even claustrophobic atmosphere produced by Colonel Beauregard's remark.

It was a question which was beginning to preoccupy Jemima Shore. She was frequently praised for her calm and quick-wittedness on television in difficult situations. For the life of her she could not think what the solution was for a situation where you arrived as the tenant of a man who turned out to be dead.

But Colonel Henry suddenly knew exactly what the protocol was.

'We must at least see that you enjoy your stay in the Highlands, Miss Shore. After this regrettable start.' He gave her an absolutely sweet smile, like a benevolent monarch. The effect of such a smile on his normally rather bleak face was delightful.

There was, then, no question of her rejection. A return to London—and Cherry—on the night train. That was the worst prospect. Jemima had not realized how much she dreaded seeing the nubile enthusiastic Cherry—before a month of recuperation was up.

Jemima, in her infinite relief, even patted Jacobite, newly returned to their side.

'And how do we get you to Eilean Fas?'

Executive problems had overcome family considerations in the Colonel's mind. 'We can take her with us, don't you think, Ossian?' he went on.

'Wouldn't look right, Colonel Henry,' said Ossian solemnly. 'Commerce before mourning.'

'You're quite right. Good point.'

'How about those dreadful hearty boys of yours? Ben, for example. Can't he help?'

'Ben! My dear Ossian, Ben has other fish to fry. Royal fish. It's the Visit. Besides, Ben and Charles . . . had you forgotten?' Colonel Henry paused and muttered. He continued more aggressively. 'And why aren't you involved, may I ask? MP and all that.'

'Oh, policy, policy,' replied Ossian airily. 'It cuts both ways. Royalty, rah, rah, on the one hand. The Red Rose, rah, rah, on the other. Most of my supporters go for both, I suspect. Much better to keep clear. Besides, I loathe tagging along—Royals, don't you know, so inclined to upstage one—so I pleaded parliamentary duties.'

'But it's the middle of August. Parliament isn't sitting,' put in Jemima. She had become interested in this amazing creature in spite of herself.

'A good MP never rests in the service of the electorate,' replied Ossian Lucas suavely.

Ten minutes later Jemima found herself sitting in the back of an enormous estate car, surrounded by her personalized luggage.

'How pretty!' said Ossian Lucas. 'Of course I prefer travelling incognito myself.' Jemima cursed Cherry.

'Probably have to have everything marked in television,' said Colonel Beauregard safely. 'Big place. I remember in the War Office—' But Ossian Lucas was already bundling him into an expensive-looking and undoubtedly foreign car.

Jemima proceeded towards Eilean Fas in the Colonel's own car. She was accompanied by Jacobite, who settled himself on top of her, and driven by Young Duncan, a retainer whose youth, it transpired, was not in his years but in his style of driving. As they left Inverness for the West, Jemima expected pigs and hens to scatter under his wheels. As it was, he challenged successfully the vast lorries and tankers of the North's oil boom.

'What a friendly dog,' observed Jemima. She felt she had to say something. 'He doesn't mind leaving his master.'

'It's Lady Edith looks after him for the most part,' commented Young Duncan. 'What with the Colonel visiting London so often for his business affairs. She's wonderful with dogs, her leddyship, trains them herself. He wouldn't be bothering you now if Lady Edith were in the car.'

'You do know the way?' Jemima said rather nervously to the left shoulder of Young Duncan.

'Aye. Ye'll be going to the Wild Island.'

'Well, Eilean Fas, actually. Is that the same?'

'Aye. Eilean Fas. The Wild Island. And a good name for it I'll be thinking. The way things have turned out.'

Young Duncan chose that moment to overtake two cars towing caravans on the main road out of Inverness. To the right of them, very close, lay the lapping waters of the Beauly Firth. It was summer, but all the same, Jemima did not fancy total immersion. Seagulls rose and screamed. She knew exactly what they meant. Seagulls welcome careless drivers.

'Puir Mr. Charles,' said Young Duncan after a pause, dramatically punctuated by feats of daring on his part, gasps from Jemima. Only Jacobite slept on unperturbed. 'Will you be going to the funeral now?'

'No, no I won't. You see we never actually met. The

Colonel will be going, I understand. It must be a great shock to him. His nephew—'

'Aye, a great shock. You could put it like that. When a mon is brought up to be puir and own nothing and suddenly in the twinkling of an eye finds himself verra verra rich. A most unexpected development.' His strong Highland accent positively lilted on the last precise words.

'Are you referring to Colonel Beauregard?' Jemima was a practised interviewer. She wanted to make no mistakes on this matter—a matter of growing interest.

'Aye, Colonel Henry as we call him hereabouts to distinguish him from Colonel Carlo, his brother who was killed in the war. Father of Mr. Charles Beauregard. A hero. Mebbe you saw the film—'

Jemima did dimly remember seeing some film. *Brother Raiders* it was called, or something equally straightforwardly swashbuckling. Henry Fonda and Kirk Douglas—was it? —played a couple of Scottish aristocrats. Brothers. One had ended by dying in the other's arms. There had been so much nonchalance about the place, with English butlers serving tea impeccably in desert tents, that she could hardly remember the intermittent bursts of heroic action. However, she was confident that all concerned—including the butler, possibly Ralph Richardson or maybe that was another film—had acquitted themselves admirably.

Jemima, however, was not interested in dead war heroes. She wanted to know more about Henry Beauregard now.

'And now I'm thinking he's inherited it all,' continued Young Duncan with a dramatic flourish.

The car had turned to the right, Duncan proceeding straight across the main road to achieve this change of direction without a pause. He drove over a narrow stone bridge. Now the car was at a halt. There was a gate before them, padlocked, three padlocks; a lodge to the left, small, stonebuilt.

Before them stretched a valley, broad but clearly defined with high mountains on either side. Glen Bronnack, valley of weeping, but looking happy enough now. Jemima knew all about it from Charles Beauregard's original letter. The road stretched forward, winding, until it vanished behind a wall of mountain. The mountains themselves were covered with dark trees, then grasses, then grass and rocks, then pure rock. There was heather—yes, it really was heather—that brilliant purple flower. The sky was still the improbably vivid blue it had been since her arrival in Scotland a few hours earlier.

There was a feeling of pristine innocence about the scene.

Once again Jemima Shore thought: this is Paradise. This is what I've come to find.

'Aye, yon's a beautiful glen true enough,' said Duncan, getting out of the car. He returned with an even older version of himself—Old Duncan perhaps?—who was unlocking the padlocked gate.

'There's many a mon would commit murder to own a bonnie glen like that,' continued Duncan. 'And those were Colonel Henry's own words to me. The very day that Mr. Charles Beauregard was drowned. And him on his way to London, and never knew the poor laddie was dead in the river.'

So saying, Young Duncan got behind the wheel again and started to drive purposefully towards Jemima's Paradise.

THREE

Nature Red

A bird rose above them into the azure sky. It seemed to hang painted above the mountains. A hawk? An eagle? Jemima knew even less about birds, she realized, than she knew about dogs.

'Colonel Henry getting the property. Of course you'd no be agreeing with all that,' observed Young Duncan. There were silver larches, she thought, or birches—anyway exquisitely beautiful trees and in such profusion, lining the road and beginning to hide the river bed. The occasional glimpse of the water showed her, however, that the gorge was deepening, the torrent increasing. The sun still shone. Jemima felt in that kind of mood when she knew that the sun would shine for ever. For her, and never mind the fact that it was Scotland. Silver and gold. The sun on the trees and dappling the water. But in patches of shadow the water was so black that she could not guess at its depth.

'You'd no agree with that,' repeated Duncan with gloomy satisfaction.

'Inherited wealth?' enquired Jemima cautiously. Experience had taught her that radically left-wing views were frequently ascribed to those who appeared on the box, without any evidence that they actually held them. Not, however, on the whole by the Duncans of this world. More by the Colonel Beauregards. She was slightly surprised to find Duncan the victim of the fashionable delusion about left-wing trendies. Jemima herself, while she had never yet voted Conservative, had years ago inherited nearly £10,000 on the deaths of both her parents in a car crash. It had bought the lease of her flat.

'Women's rights, now. That's what you'll be for, I'll be thinking. My wife watched your programme the other night. She found it most instructive.'

The road was starting to ascend and curve at the same time. Duncan warmed to his theme, and turning his head on the word 'instructive,' produced a dramatic roll of the car. It was not, Jemima felt, an ideal time for the discussion of women's rights.'

'So you'll be thinking Miss Clementina Beauregard should inherit the property,' continued Duncan, nodding vigorously and slewing the wheel to navigate a particularly sudden corner. 'And so will she be thinking the same, I'll be bound. And so will she.'

He cackled. There was no other word for it. 'And there'll be others thinking that on the Estate too, mind you. Colonel Henry is a fine gentleman. I'm no saying any different. But there will be those saying that it should go to the lass all the same. Seeing as her father Colonel Carlo, who was a hero, as I was telling you, built the Estate up when he was young, and her mother, who was an American lady, verra rich, the sort they have over there, made it all into such a fine place.'

Jemima made a sympathetic noise. She was now looking over the tops of the larches. The bird, her bird, still hovered in the sky. She had no idea of its height.

'Ah the puir wee girl,' said Duncan, turning his head again to look at Jemima and adopting a sentimental tone rather different from his normally precise Scottish utterance. 'To lose her brother and home and all, in one fearful day. It's no wonder she's become a little touched.'

'Touched?' And now there was another bird. Twisting and turning with its pair.

'Barricading herself in. Says she won't give up the Castle to the devil himself. And worse. Aye, the language of the lasses these days. It's the television of course.' Aware of his solecism Duncan continued hurriedly, 'Or so my wife says. But I say they have to learn it somewhere and you can hear worse in Glasgow any Saturday night. As I was saying, Miss Clementina is possessed of Colonel Carlo's guns there. The famous Beauregard Armoury. You'll have heard of that now, Miss?'

Jemima shook her head.

Guns did not interest her, nor did shooting as a sport. Although it was August, and judging from the gun-cases on the platform at Inverness there was a good deal of it around, she had no intention of joining in anything so lethal herself. Fishing—now that was a sport for a detached and contemplative soul in a Highland environment.

I don't know whether you are a fisherwoman [*Charles Beauregard had written in his original letter*], but there is not much fishing at Eilean Fas. It's also rather dangerous in places. You have to watch your step . . . Still, Bonnie Prince Charlie is said to have enjoyed the fishing at Eilean Fas, according to the legend. We even have a 14 lb. stuffed salmon in a case at the Castle and firmly labelled 'Caught by HRH Prince Charles Edward Stuart (HM King Charles III of Scotland) April 15, 1746.' That was Mother's doing. The only question was whether she caught the fish herself on the home beat or got the ghillie to do it for her. The Eilean Fas story has to be nonsense because no one has caught a salmon off the island in years, in spite of many efforts to do so. The river is too deep and too fast. The Estate Office will give you a prize of £100 if you do. Then we can put up the rent.

Memories of that original rather jolly letter reminded Jemima that she had quite looked forward to meeting Charles Beauregard. If not for too long or too often. Drowned. She wondered suddenly how and where he had been drowned. Not fishing, she hoped, in the dangerous water off Eilean Fas. Jemima shivered, and fixed her eyes once more on the pair of birds hovering and fluttering. Even as she watched, one of the pair made an astoundingly sharp, almost vertical dive to the ground. She very much hoped it was not a bird of prey.

Dogs, guns and even birds belonged to a side of country life of which she knew little. It was certainly not nature red in tooth and claw which she had come to appreciate, but Paradise, a primitive untouched Eden, a kind of Scottish Forest of Arden, in which Young Duncan could perhaps be Touchstone (a Touchstone who watched telly). She would perhaps be Rosalind in her beige doublet and hose.

Rosalind—come to think of it, Miss Clementina Beauregard was probably the true Rosalind round here. Wasn't the original plot of As You Like It, as far as she could recall, the dispossession of Rosalind by her father's brother? At least this Miss Beauregard was a woman of spirit. Barricading herself in indeed! Rosalind had merely taken herself off to the Forest of Arden.

Duncan swerved, apparently to avoid a rabbit. But it turned out he had swerved in order to kill it.

'Diseased. Best dead,' he said briefly.

'But not us,' Jemima wanted to add. The swerve had brought them perilously near the precipice. She thanked her lucky stars that the road through Glen Bronnack, the Valley of Weeping, had proved empty indeed. A car coming the other way would surely have been fatal. Perhaps the road was treated like a single-line railway track? With only one car on the stretch at a time.

The car screeched to a halt. They were on the very corner of the steepest turn yet.

'There, do you see it now?' cried Duncan with enormous satisfaction. To her absolute horror, Jemima saw beside the road the carcase of what had once doubtlessly been a sheep. Surely, he couldn't be—

But Duncan was gazing at the new view before him. He must have seen it—she had no idea—a thousand times, ten thousand times if he had been brought up here, but Duncan was gazing at the prospect before him with all the wonder and delight of some Highland Cortés.

The final corner had brought them into a different terrain. It was as if they had passed through a mountain barrier or pass. Below them the land dropped away down to the river. Above them still soared the mountainside, with its trees running up to the stone level, then halting. But Jemima's attention was concentrated on the new fertility of this plain, the winding placid pattern of the river, looking like something in a mediaeval psalter in which the figure of a pilgrim might be seen at various stages of his journey. In the centre of this valley the river broadened out into a wide lake, on which could be seen pine trees, rhododendrons, other bushes more domestic than wild. Overlooking all this romantic perfection in which the sun still shone with a remorseless brightness out of its blue sky—so that she was beginning to feel she was in Greece rather than the Highlands of Scotland—was a gigantic Victorian castle.

Be-turreted and be-pinnacled, it dominated the landscape. It also looked exactly like a castle in a fairy story, from which the boy adventurer might try to rescue the princess. There was much of fantasy, nothing rough, bleak or mediaeval about it. In fact it was not even grey, like the Scottish stones surrounding it, but red, rich dark red.

Castle Beauregard: a nineteenth-century structure. A previous edifice on the same site was visited by Bonnie Prince Charlie in the course of his peregrinations round the Highlands—at any rate according to the *Northern Guide*. '*Oui, c'est un beau regard,*' he was supposed to have observed to some ancestor of her host's at the time. What appreciation of natural beauty historical royalty always managed to fit into the busiest schedule, and how they preserved their gracious royal good humour in the tightest corner . . .

If the view itself was tranquil, there was nothing particularly peaceful about the structure of this castle. From every red turret seemed to spring another turret like a series of acrobats. Even the pinnacles gave you the impression that, like some form of life, they might be spawning and proliferating while your back was turned. One large central layer appeared to occupy the role of keep. There was a flagpole on the highest turret and a flag which, however, was not stirring in the windless day.

'A fine property!' said Duncan with undisguised approval, smacking or rather chewing his lips. 'There's many Glasgow businessmen, or them from the South, would pay a fine price for it. An Arab, mebbe, looking for a place for his harem.'

Well, thought Jemima, that's one way of putting it. That's how he measures his approval.

'You can't blame a lass for wanting to hold onto it, now, can you?' went on Duncan.

In the foreground Jemima suddenly noticed a small whitewashed church, oblong, like a child's building brick. Arranged neatly around it were some grey stone graves. And a very high fence. The fence looked old.

'That barrier,' she enquired. 'So high—?'

'The church you'll be meaning. Oh, it's the deer come and eat the flowers,' said Duncan briefly. 'They're unco' fond of flowers, deers. And young trees. You'll find that quick enough on Eilean Fas.'

Jemima thought poetically she would enjoy the acquaintance of the deer on Eilean Fas. As wild creatures, they were welcome to the inappropriate flowers of civilization as far as she was concerned.

But the church—and this was the day of Charles Beauregard's funeral, as she had already discovered to her cost. Was he to be buried here? Presumably Colonel Henry and Ossian Lucas had talked of the Glen Bronnack church. And would Miss Clementina Beauregard, then, not be attending, barricaded within her be-turreted fortress? She must have a pleasant vista for a siege.

Jemima was still meditating on the prospect before her, framed by the purple mountains at the head of the valley, a few of them snow-capped despite the season, when the car screeched to a halt. For a moment she thought that Duncan had actually hit something. Then she realized that they had been quite literally waved down.

A young man with a flag had, as it seemed, appeared suddenly out of the hillside itself, and Duncan had had to brake sharply in order to avoid hitting him.

Jemima gazed at the flag, which was made easy for her by the fact that the young man in question was now holding it aloft. Like the graffiti at Inverness Station, it was emblazoned in scarlet, with the same obscure emblem beneath. 'Up the Red Rose,' it proclaimed.

'Up the Red Rose,' repeated the flag-bearer.

'And may the Red run White,' replied Young Duncan with great fervour.

FOUR

Blood on the Rose

Slowly, Jemima took a measured look at the flag-bearer.

He was in fact an extremely young man. He had the black curly hair and blue eyes, the kind of bull-like looks traditionally associated with Ireland. He was wearing a kilt, and a white T-shirt on which a large red rose was emblazoned—or perhaps splashed would have been a better word—for there were splashes of red emanating from the rose. It took her a moment to realize that the rose was in fact intended to be dripping blood. Beneath the rose, also in the colour of blood, was the emblem which she had noticed on the station platform.

And behind the man's ear—improbable touch—was a real red rose. The shirt was pristine. But the flower was overblown and slightly wilting. Jemima did not think it would survive many more expeditions of this sort.

'Up the Red Rose,' repeated this unlikely dandy, shaking his flag. His expression was quite amiable.

'If you say so.' To her own ears Jemima's voice sounded over-gracious.

'And may the Red run White,' joined in Duncan for the second time.

'Quite correct. Ah, Mr. Duncan, it's you driving, is it? I thought mebbe it would be Sandy.' There was a pause. 'And you'll be Miss Jemima Shore?'

There seemed no point in denying it.

'Yes, I'm Jemima Shore. And who might you be?'

'He's Lachlan Stuart from Torran,' said Duncan.

'Captain Lachlan, ADC to the Chief of the Red Rose.'

'Captain Stuart, why don't you lower the flag,' said Jemima persuasively. She was happy to give him his military rank. Captain Stuart. Captain Shore. She thought for an instant of her father. A very different kind of military man. More like Colonel Beauregard, as glimpsed in the Railway Hotel. The image vanished. She went on, 'And then we can talk.'

Captain Stuart seemed a harmless enough crank, Scottish style.

'Aye, it will be a pleasure to talk to you,' said Captain Stuart. 'A guid talk. I've a guid deal to tell you of the greatest interest. Never you fear. But no just now. Just now I'm inviting you on behalf of the Red Rose to view the coffin of his Majesty.' This flummoxed Jemima completely. The coffin of his Majesty. Were there two coffins? Was the Glen full of coffins? No, that was going too far, even in this fantastic world in which she found herself.

'Mr. Charles Beauregard's coffin . . .' she began cautiously.

'The coffin of his late Majesty King Charles Edward of Scotland. Who you'll mebbe be knowing by the name of Charles Beauregard,' replied Captain Stuart, drawing himself up into a passable military pose.

Heaven have mercy, thought Jemima. What on earth was he talking about? She wished she had a firmer grasp on Scottish history, to know what on earth Captain Stuart could be meaning, with his reference to majesties and kings. Scottish history was an absolutely closed book to Jemima apart from a few salient points like the '45. She had been busy studying Scottish topography for her holiday, and had brought with her the poems of Burns and a couple of Walter Scotts in paperback. The Burns—the love poems—had been a present from Guthrie Carlyle. He had inscribed it: 'Maybe you will invite me to your island...' Jemima had accepted the book and made a mental resolution to do no such thing. The Scotts on the other hand, *Old Mortality* and *The Heart of Midlothian*, had been recommended to her as 'the good Scotts'—as though there could be bad Scotts like bad people—by Marigold Milton, her brilliant if didactic girlfriend from Cambridge days, now suitably teaching English to a widening circle of terrorized but fascinated students at London University. Neither Burns nor Scott, national heroes as they might be, struck her as likely to be particularly helpful in the present situation.

It seemed that she should have been studying the ancestry of the Scottish royal family. There was some kind of Stuart pretender; she dimly recalled ceremonies in which, surely, a white rose rather than a red had been involved. But wasn't the fellow a Bavarian prince anyway?

Of course it was up to her whether she chose to discover the answer to these questions. She imagined she was perfectly free to refuse Captain Lachlan's courteous invitation on behalf of the Red Rose. She would simply express her wish to reach her destination as soon as possible (true enough) and pass by on the other side from the flag-waving self-styled ADC to the Chief... Curiosity, at once her best and her worst quality, got the better of her. The funeral was hardly likely to last long, and she was keen to satisfy a certain low desire to find out more about this surprising Beauregard family in a painless manner.

But with Lachlan installed in the front seat of the car, she discovered almost immediately that she was wrong on one count: the funeral was not intended to be brief.

'We intend to see that the late monarch gets a full royal funeral,' explained Captain Stuart. 'As far as possible in the present circumstances. And will ye be driving with more care, Mr. Duncan. We don't want anything to happen to Miss Shore while she's under the protection of the Red Rose.'

Well, thought Jemima, he may be a Royalist nut, but at least we agree about Duncan's hair-raising driving...

'So you got yourself a job, did you, now? An ADC, do you call it?' countered Duncan sarcastically to the quip about his driving. 'After you were thrown off the Estate.' But he did slow down his driving, Jemima noticed.

Lachlan Stuart gave Duncan an extremely dirty look. Jemima thought it wise to intervene.

'Look here, Captain Stuart—'

'Captain Lachlan, if you please, Miss Shore. We have no surnames in the Army of the Red Rose. For security reasons, you understand.'

Security with regard to surnames was surely an idle matter, with Duncan there to provide the necessary information, like a vindictive chorus. Nevertheless Jemima was not disposed to argue the point.

'Captain Lachlan, what on earth is my part in all this? I'm simply on my way to Eilean Fas—'

'Aye, we know that. We had the information from the Castle.'

'From whom?' He ignored the question.

'And we're taking you along purely as an observer.'

'But an observer of what—'

'Why, to tell the world of the royal funeral of his late

majesty. You'll be representing the world's press and television. And then we'll let you go to make your report. It'll be the making of your career, mebbe,' added Captain Lachlan kindly, 'to have such an opportunity.'

Curiouser and curiouser. Madder and madder. The press and television indeed! Did he imagine that she carried television cameras with her, somehow concealed in her expensive luggage, to say nothing of travelling crews.

'And what's the Colonel going to say to all this? And Mr. Lucas the MP, all the way from London?' enquired Duncan gleefully. It was a question which had been vaguely worrying Jemima.

'The usurper, Colonel Beauregard as you call him, won't get here. By orders of the Red Rose,' responded Captain Lachlan confidently. 'My men are posted further down the road.'

'He was the Colonel to you quick enough. When you worked on the Estate,' Duncan put in in his sing-song voice, apparently unable to resist intervening.

'There's blood on the Red Rose now, Mr. Duncan,' answered Captain Lachlan with intensity. 'You know that. Everyone on the Estate—as you call it, but I've another name for it—everyone knows that. Who killed Mr. Charles Beauregard? Tell me that now. Never tell me he drowned. Him knowing the river all ways since he was a boy. Who would go fishing in Marjorie's Pool? Just when he was setting up the memorial and all?'

Duncan said nothing. His silence worried Jemima more than the presumably wild accusations of Lachlan Stuart. She had expected him to rebut them furiously. But he said nothing.

'And where was Mr. Ben Beauregard on that occasion? Fishing down the river…His own cousin, and who hated him since they were boys—' Captain Lachlan stopped. There had been genuine emotion in his voice. He seemed ashamed of having expressed it.

'Drowned,' he repeated much more calmly. 'Aye, there's blood on the Red Rose.'

Duncan's only response was to drive faster as though to get away from Captain Lachlan's passion.

'Mr Duncan, I warned you,' said Captain Lachlan after a brief silence. 'The Red Rose wouldna like it if anything was to happen to Miss Jemima Shore.'

The road was descending into the plain. It seemed appropriate that the brilliant sun, coruscating on the waters of the loch, and which had accompanied Jemima since her arrival in Scotland, had now disappeared. Clouds were massing at the head of the valley. The heads of the high peaks had vanished. Even the heather had lost its vivid purple. How very sombre was its colour without the sun, she thought. And mountains, so often allegedly blue, were actually grey, anthracite grey, or even something darker. The loch, reflecting the sky, had not so much lost its colour as gained an angry positive darkness.

By the time they reached the simple white-washed church, there was no feeling of light or sun in the valley at all.

Standing round the church were a group of men. Some wore dark clothes, but the majority wore kilts with dark jackets. She noticed that no one wore a T-shirt splashed with blood on the rose. These were presumably the mourners for Charles Beauregard. There were no women outside the church that Jemima could see. Above the church there was a small white arch with a bell inside it. And above that was a flag. In the gathering breeze, the flag stirred and fluttered. On a white background, a vast rose could be clearly seen. There seemed to be some royal arms of sorts there as well. Below that the red emblem—UR2. Of course. Up the Red Rose. Jemima had always been rather good at guessing riddles.

Now she saw that the mourners outside the church all had red roses in their buttonholes.

Where was the rest of the congregation—the Beauregard family? Jemima suddenly felt rather ill-equipped to attend this strange funeral and regretted the half-frivolous impulse which had brought her to the church.

With his debonair courtesy, Captain Lachlan ushered Jemima up the gravel path through the small lych-gate. Church of St. Margaret and All the Angels, Glen Bronnack. Mass 8 am daily; 8 and 11.30 Sundays. For the first time Jemima realized that this plain little valley structure was in fact a Catholic church. Its plainness had deceived her. How very different from the ornate chapel of the Convent of the Blessed Eleanor where she, as a Protestant living nearby, had been educated during the war.

Jemima suddenly wished passionately that she had Mother Agnes by her side. Mother Agnes, the young but increasingly formidable Reverend Mother of that convent, was, she often thought, the only truly serene person that she knew. Her serenity added to her strength. Mother Agnes would know how to deal with Lachlan, of that she was quite convinced. Lacking the nun at her side, Jemima tried to imagine at least how Mother Agnes would behave in these circumstances. Calm, but forceful calm, seemed to be the watchword. As it was, she would have to content herself relating it all to Mother Agnes afterwards in a long, long letter once she had reached Eilean Fas. And peace.

There were graves on either side of the path. Most of them looked old, forgotten, mossy. But one newly dug, surrounded by red roses, caught her attention. Beyond, surrounded by a little low hedge of green bush, was a separate enclave. Here were situated a number of graves. All very freshly tended. No moss here. And there, quite clearly to her surprise, was another freshly dug grave. By its side, also, was grouped a flowershop of wreaths, white chrysanthemums, touches of yellow, predominantly white flowers. Conventional funeral floristry. And not a sign of a red rose to be seen.

Still gallant, Captain Lachlan ushered Jemima to the front door of the church. As Jemima entered the church itself, heads, a multitude of them, or so it seemed, turned round, as though according to a single command. A blur of white faces, all quite unknown to her, all looking as reproachful as a herd of sheep in a field disturbed from grazing by a strange dog.

The small church was packed. The walls, like its exterior, were white-washed, and punctuated here and there by brass plates and other memorial stones. The Stations of the Cross were there to remind one of its Catholicism, otherwise it resembled a simple Scottish church of some lower denomination much more than any Catholic church Jemima had ever visited. But there was an extraordinary glass window above the altar. Greens and blues swam in front of her eyes like a lighted aquarium. Figures, knights on horses—perhaps crusaders—swirled among the vivid colours in what was some kind of battle scene. Gazing at it a moment, Jemima lost all sense of her surroundings.

The next moment a rich harsh voice rang out in a very strong and—for once—ugly Scottish accent:

'Lachlan Stuart, you have no right to bring your wicked flummery into the House of God. You are making a mockery of Christian burial.'

The sheep-like faces of the congregation continued to stare in their direction. Striding down the aisle towards them was a truly enormous man, his long black cassock flapping behind him. Over it, the white surplice hardly seemed to come halfway down. Thick black eyebrows, in contrast to the shock of white hair above, dominated the face above the surplice. The man must be at least six and a half feet tall, thought Jemima. And he was gazing at Captain Lachlan with blazing fury. Jemima herself got a scathing look. Of all the absurd things, she was suddenly embarrassed to find herself wearing trousers in church.

'And, wummun, whomsoever you may be, will you not cover your head decently in the House of God? And in the presence of the dead.'

It was then that Jemima became aware of the coffin, draped in black velvet, behind the priest. An enormous wreath of red roses was centred on top of the black velvet. There was a surround of some kind of tartan, and tartan flags were hanging from poles at each corner of the coffin. Her eyes travelled to the altar. Once again red roses—that most unlikely accompaniment to a funeral—were here placed, defiantly as it were, in vast vases.

Jemima felt in her handbag. It was no time to be arguing about the relaxation of the Church's rules concerning head-covering. Which as far as she knew had occurred many years back in the rest of the world, but news of which had evidently not penetrated Glen Bronnack. A chiffon scarf, Hanae Mori, printed with a design of hearts, emerged and fluttered nervously in her fingers as she tried to tie it rapidly over her hair. Its pale pretty colours must make her, she thought, look even more unsuitable among the sea of black hats and veils which stretched before her.

Captain Lachlan himself was in no way discomposed by the priest's anger.

'Father Flanagan, you may now proceed with the funeral of his late Majesty,' was all he said, with a calm Jemima envied.

'I will not be burying Mr. Charles Beauregard under such flags and roses and the like,' replied Father Flanagan fiercely. 'I said it to his face when he was alive and I'll not be holding my tongue when he's dead. I denounce the Red

Rose and all its works. An insult to the dead, and to Almighty God and to his sorrowing family.'

'Are you referring to me, Father?' said a clear female voice from somewhere above their heads. Jemima realized for the first time that there was a gallery in the plain church. She looked back. The gallery, which ran the width of the church, over its doorway, was totally empty except for one girl, sitting in the centre on what looked remarkably like a kind of wooden throne.

'Since I am the only member of this family sorrowing over the death of Charles Beauregard, it is my request that the Red Rose is present,' continued the high clear voice. 'I instruct you, Father, to proceed with my brother's funeral.' She paused, and looked furiously, disdainfully, at the rest of the congregation below her. 'I regard the rest of you, as you well know, as murderers.'

'Her Majesty Queen Clementina,' murmured Captain Lachlan with something like reverence. He even managed a kind of bow.

'Murderers,' repeated Miss Clementina Beauregard.

Dead But Not Buried

There was a kind of commotion in the little church, a subdued but audible buzz of horror. Jemima dropped her eyes from the improbable figure of vengeance in the gallery, and tried to form some impression of the members of the congregation as individuals.

The general image of the congregation was now dissolving into a series of portraits. Miss Clementina Beauregard was already a portrait in her own right. Or rather, sitting there, with her long fair hair under a black velvet beret and her black clothes with white frills at the neck, she had the air of a mermaid in mourning. What was that Hans Andersen story about a little mermaid who walked on knives to gain the man she loved . . . Clementina Beauregard would have done well as a mourning mermaid. Cold, even in her sorrow.

The rest of the congregation did not look as though they had come out of any sort of fairy story. They were

neither fey nor frail in appearance. Or to put it another
way, they were positively beefy-looking. What you might
expect in a Scottish church of any denomination on a
Sunday. Except that this wasn't Sunday, and Jemima was
reluctantly coming to the conclusion that nothing in
Scotland was going to be quite as she had expected.

The front left-hand pew had an obvious gap at its end.
That, she guessed, was for the absent Colonel Henry to
slip into. And it was likely now to remain empty. The
woman who actually headed the row was wearing a conventional black hat. She continued to stare persistently in
the direction of Clementina and her gallery.

The Colonel's lady? Presumably. It was an unexpectedly
sweet face, with those kind of features—small nose, round
chin—which time blurs, removing the prettiness of youth,
leaving behind something slightly pathetic, distressed, in
its place. 'Remember me, I was young and pretty once.' A
tall young man standing next to her put his arm round her
shoulders, stooping to do so. She turned her head, in its
small black hat, to look at him. What a preponderance of
males there was in this church on a closer inspection.
There was no female in the family pew, with the excep-
tion of this middle-aged woman; then of course there was
the galleried Clementina. At that moment a boy leant
forward in the front pew and touched the woman on her
arm. He had a fresh rather cheeky face, pink cheeks and
black hair; he looked quite cheerful. Not much funereal
pretence here. And then Jemima distinctly saw him give
his mother, if that was who she was, a thumbs-up sign. He
even smiled broadly. No, no funereal pretence here,
whatsoever.

The woman turned her face once more to the gallery.
Something about her expression arrested Jemima's attention. There was real feeling here. Alone of the staring
faces, she seemed to display not so much anger, embarrass-

ment or real outrage as some other emotion. Compassion, perhaps.

The tall young man whispered in her ear. His expression was quite stern. Jemima would remember that face. How tall they all were—and not every one of those beefy young men could be Beauregards.

The tallest man in the church was, however, Father Flanagan. The priest had not deigned to reply to Clementina Beauregard. He stood for a moment, a huge and rather frightening figure. Then he too turned and strode back up the aisle. Captain Lachlan handed Jemima into a back pew with his usual grace. The sheeplike faces were now all turned towards the altar.

To her continued amazement Jemima Shore, at eleven o'clock on an August morning, found herself attending a Roman Catholic Requiem Mass in a remote Highland church, for a man she had never met. By this time, in her romantic anticipation of her holiday, she had expected to be sitting tranquilly on her lonely island gazing at peaty waters, admiring the heather. Alone. As it was, she was beginning to think wryly that Megalithic House, that busy hive of television, was a better bet for solitude than the Highlands of Scotland.

The Mass proceeded.

Yes, she would certainly have something to write to Reverend Mother Agnes about.

In fact the Mass now proceeded quietly, almost quickly. There was no sermon or address of any sort, either from Father Flanagan or Captain Lachlan, which perhaps under the circumstances was just as well. There was no drama about it at all, except what Mother Agnes would call the central drama of the Mass itself.

Holy Communion. Members of the Beauregard family filed up to the altar. Jemima realized that in spite of those far-off years as Protestant day-girl at a Catholic convent, and in spite of recent traumatic experiences at the same convent, she had never actually attended a Catholic Requiem before. She was faintly surprised to see that communion played some part in it. The front phalanx of mourners left the front pew for the communion rails looking more like bullocks, and less like sheep.

But from the gallery Clementina Beauregard did not descend. Nor for that matter did Captain Lachlan leave his pew for the communion rails. It was only at the end of the requiem that Captain Lachlan made any move at all.

Then he looked up in the direction of Clementina Beauregard. She nodded. Lachlan made a gesture, once again courteous—a positively chivalrous man. Four men in dark jackets, wearing the kilt, red roses in their button-holes, stepped forward to the corners of the coffin.

There was a faint gasp from someone—it sounded like 'Oh no'—as the four men shouldered the box. Somewhere someone wept. A woman. That vulnerable compassionate woman perhaps.

Under the implacable gaze of Miss Clementina Beauregard, the coffin, in its black coverlet, still crowned with its red roses, was marched slowly out of the church.

Lachlan, motioning Jemima to follow him, fell in behind it.

'Ye'll now see the royal burial, a verra wonderful sight which the Red Rose has brought you here to witness,' he whispered. Jemima pulled off her headscarf. As she did so, she noticed a man entering the church by the side door; if he was a member of the Red Rose, he wore neither T-shirt nor flower behind his ear. The most violent splash of colour about him was his shock of bright red hair. He spoke urgently in Lachlan's ear, as though remonstrating with him. Lachlan shook his head. The red-haired man looked angry or at least discomposed; then he vanished again through the side door. Jemima and Lachlan left the church together.

No doubt the royal burial would have been a very wonderful sight. Who could tell?—since the sight that met their eyes as they left the church was totally unexpected.

Dark-suited as before, but somehow grown in stature or at least in authority since that encounter at Inverness Station, Colonel Henry Beauregard confronted them. He was flanked by a number of men—six or more—whose clothes seemed to indicate that in contrast to the forces of the Red Rose, they had not planned on attending a funeral that day. Two of the men were wearing boots, thick green boots; one wore a dark waterproof jacket; there were tweed jackets, dark brownish tweed the colour of peat, jerseys. One man even wore a tweed hat. There was no sign of Mr. Ossian Lucas MP.

'Ah, Stuart,' said the Colonel easily. 'Just get your fellows to put down that coffin, would you?'

He might have been talking to the barman of a West End club, asking him to put down a whiskey on the table. It was an authoritarian voice. But it was not loud.

To Jemima it all seemed totally unreal. The nonchalance of the Colonel's attitude added to the unreality. Lachlan hesitated: he looked round. Jemima had the impression that he might have been looking for his red-haired companion. But there was no sign of him.

'Her Majesty Queen Clementina—' he began bravely.

'I don't want a scene in front of the church,' said the Colonel. His tone was still easy.

'Do as he says, Lachlan,' said a voice behind her.

'Mr. Rory—' Lachlan was undoubtedly losing confidence.

'I don't need any help to deal with this,' said the Colonel. The tall young man looked abashed.

Lachlan still hesitated: finally he gave a quick, rather

ungracious signal to the four pallbearers of the Red Rose who were motionless with the coffin on their shoulders.

'Aye, we'll be gone now, Colonel,' he said sullenly. 'But we'll be back. And we'll have our rights too. The Wild Island for a royal memorial. You'll see.'

Slowly, glumly, the members of the Red Rose lowered the coffin to the ground. But it was not the Colonel's motley force which now shouldered it.

'Rory, Hamish, Gavin, Niall,' said the Colonel in a much sharper voice. This time he sounded as if he was talking not to a barman, but to four dogs. And like dogs, four of the healthiest looking young men Jemima had ever seen bounded forward with ruddy cheeks, eager eyes. Just like dogs. Even the tall Rory now looked eager rather than sulky. None of them possessed an iota of the distinction of the Colonel. Their features were somehow coarsened with too much health—or was it youth? His were refined by age—or was it authority? For the second time that day, Jemima thought of her father. As she had seen him in her childhood's eye. Not the sad father of the postwar years, but the magnificent military man of her infancy.

All the same, for all her thoughts of her own father, it came as a surprise to hear one of these amiable boys say:

'Which graveyard, Dad?'

Dad. It did not sound appropriate.

'The family graveyard,' replied the Colonel in a clipped voice. 'Where else?'

'But they were digging a sort of royal grave, covered in red roses.'

'Don't be more ridiculous than you can help, Hamish,' was all the Colonel said.

'Clementina said—'

'The family graveyard,' repeated the Colonel. There was thunder, not too distant, in his voice. Hamish dropped back.

The boys proceeded with the coffin towards the family graveyard. The former coffinbearers, relieved of their burden and led by Lachlan, were shambling away down the road. Nobody seemed to pay much attention to them. The Glen swallowed them up.

'Ah, Miss Shore.' It was the Colonel again, in an exceptionally affable mood. 'Awfully sorry to have got you mixed up in all this. Just a little local difficulty. As Harold Macmillan would say.'

Jemima smiled. She did not need to be told the source of the quotation.

'Look, we'll just get this sad business *over*. And then I'll drive you to Eilean Fas myself. I don't want,' said the Colonel carefully, 'you to think we are complete barbarians.'

'Oh, please—' said Jemima, with a regal wave of her hand. She was still aware that she was waving away a great deal. But the Colonel's courtly manners aroused that sort of response in her.

The coffin was being lowered into the family grave. The mourners stood around. Then a woman's breathless voice said:

'Henry, you must *do* something—' For one second the Colonel frowned, a truly terrifying split-second frown. Then he continued in his usual calm way:

'My dear,' he said, 'may I present my wife? Miss Jemima Shore, my wife, Edith.'

'Henry,' went on the woman, and it was that vulnerable woman of the front pew, 'you must do something about Clementina. She won't come to the burial if you're there. I said: Poor Charles is dead, there's no point in arguing now. We can't bring him back to life. She said: Dead but not buried. In that fearfully cold voice of hers. Just like Leonie's in one of her icy moods. She's saying you murdered Charles.'

The Colonel still sounded absolutely calm.

'How utterly absurd of her, my dear. And rather absurd of you, Edith, to repeat it.' He turned away from his wife's flushed face, her hair untidy under its confining hat.

'Miss Shore, perhaps you would prefer to stay in the car, while we sort all this out.'

It was definitely a command, for all the politeness. Jemima was glad to obey. She walked down the gravel path to Duncan's car. Ahead of her lay the loch, dark grey anthracite. Rain was beginning to beat down on the edges of the water. At that moment she narrowly missed being knocked down by a sports car, white, driven very fast. At the wheel she recognized the black beret, fair hair and pale set face of Clementina Beauregard.

She had kept her word not to attend the funeral of her brother, in the presence of her uncle. What had she said of Charles Beauregard? Dead—but not buried. It seemed an ominous start to a holiday that was to take place, willy-nilly, in the bosom of the Beauregard family territory.

SIX

Island of Eden

'No chance of strangers here, you see,' said Colonel Henry. It was half an hour later. By now the estate car was swaying over the narrow bridge to the Wild Island. The bridge had evidently been built of a series of wooden slats. A good many of these were now missing. The remaining slats shifted and seemed to complain under the car's weight.

It really was an astonishingly narrow bridge. Not even a parapet or a handrail. Two sagging ropes on either side. Hardly sufficient to safeguard a person, let alone a car. Had there ever been a crash here? Jemima shivered. She shot a look at Colonel Henry's handsome hawk-like profile—how narrow his lips were—and did not like to ask.

Beneath them the water looked as black as the loch. On the left the cliffs of the Wild Island reared up, enormously high. Below the bridge, forking down to the loch, the river was deep and fast-flowing. A wide river with vast trees lining the edges of it, huge and very dark green trees whose roots must surely be in the river itself as their branches trailed in the water. Jemima thought of trees drawn by Arthur Rackham. These trees too looked menacing. There were no banks to this river, no footholds if an unwary traveller slipped into the dark waters. Something seemed to jump there below. Jump and splash. A fish? A salmon? But Charles Beauregard had said there were no salmon to be caught here, by tradition. The surface of the river recovered its smoothness.

It was still raining. Jemima looked away from the threatening trees upstream and caught her breath.

The river above the bridge was no river, but a vast waterfall caught between two rocks, forced through a chasm. The effect was startling, the pounding water as it poured down looking yellow, its spray white.

Her exclamation had caught the attention of the Colonel.

'The Fair Falls,' he said briefly.

'Fair?' The falls looked dark, neither fair of aspect nor intention, to Jemima.

'Watchful. The watchers' falls. The guardians, if you like. Guardians of the Wild Island. They are literally its guardians, you see. The falls prevent anyone crossing to the island except by this bridge.' Colonel Henry sounded more complacent than the occasion warranted.

'They could swim . . . ' said Jemima doubtfully. She was fond of swimming herself. She remembered foolishly that she had packed a printed leopard-skin two-piece costume, bought in New York: in fact, to be honest, a bikini. Packing in her London flat, a dip in a Scottish burn from a cottage surrounded by water had seemed quite plausible. It now seemed an utterly ridiculous concept. She could not possibly imagine herself immersed in these black inhospitable waters, so turbulent, so restless.

Colonel Henry had rattled off the bridge onto the island itself.

'A Canadian once tried to shoot these rapids,' he said conversationally. 'In a canoe. To prove it could be done. In the war.'

'I gather it's impossible.'

'Oh, absolutely. As a matter of fact his head hit a rock on the way down. He's buried in the churchyard. The idea was quite ridiculous from the start.'

Jemima could think of no comment to make. It was all a very long time ago: during the war, when men were dying everywhere. And some of them under the gallant command of Colonel Henry. All the same there seemed a singular lack of regret in the recollection. The fellow had failed—and had been a fool into the bargain.

She turned her attention to the steep road—if it could be called that—which they were now climbing. It wound upwards, heavily banked by what looked like rhododendrons. Pines, Scotch firs, whatever they were, and some massive oaks poked their heads out of the shrubberies. How beautiful it must look in the spring, if all these green shrubs flowered.

Now in high summer everything was green; green and heavy. Dank even, in the rain. And so many different greens, the black green of the firs; the light pretty feminine green of the larches; the grey-green of the oak trunks. But always green. It might have been some tropical scene in a Rousseau picture, except for the cold. There was nothing tropical about the temperature. Jemima was genuinely shivering now and longed for her faithful white Burberry raincoat.

There was no heather here, no stone, no flowers. Only green. Tigers or leopards might come forth from this jungle. And at that moment, even as the thought crossed her mind, a small deer broke out of the undergrowth on her left. The perfect miniature bounding creature had a Walt Disney quality.

To her amazement, Colonel Henry immediately and purposefully drove straight towards the deer.

'Little bugger,' he said, missing it. Then by way of explanation: 'Roe deer, you know. They eat the tops of the trees.' To Jemima, frankly, it did not seem sufficient explanation. She wondered suddenly if Colonel Henry was prone to the elimination of young animals. Those which stood in his way, that is.

But at that moment the sight of the house stopped her voice, and her thoughts. It was all so totally unexpected. Hardly a house, certainly not a cottage, more like a church. It was built of louring grey stone, in contrast to the rich red of Castle Beauregard, with long high-arched windows.

And below the house, equally surprising, falling away, stone terraces, overgrown with grass, but still showing traces of magnificence; more rhododendrons, and a view. A view which was open and grandiose: the river below them, the mountains beyond. Above their heads loomed another mountain. Beyond them, the chasm. And at that very moment, as they arrived, the sun came out. The rain did not stop. So that when Jemima first saw Tigh Fas, with its stone porch, church-like aspect and all, it was framed in the halo of a rainbow.

'It's so absolutely—surprising,' she said after a moment. She was aware of the banality of her comment. But she could think of nothing more appropriate to say.

'We get a lot of rainbows round here,' replied Colonel Henry. Once again he sounded complacent, as though he were personally responsible for them.

'I meant the house. Is this the house? This is Tigh Fas?

You see, I had expected a cottage.' Her own letter, Cherry's letter, had specified a cottage. She had *wanted* a cottage.

'Of course this is Tigh Fas,' Colonel Henry sounded surprised. 'I must say it's not exactly my idea of a cottage. Don't know what your standards are in television of course.' He shot her a doubtful look as if anything was to be expected from this unknown medium. 'As a matter of fact we'd call it a shooting lodge up here. My grandmother built it, when she first came to the Glen as a bride, before she got around to rebuilding the Castle. But there's always been some kind of dwelling on Eilean Fas: natural defensive position. Bonnie Prince Charlie is said to have rested up here after the fiasco of the '45. Believe he had a thoroughly good time.' The Colonel spoke as though the Prince had been a recent tenant.

Bonnie Prince Charlie may have been happy about his let, thought Jemima crossly, but I am not. Besides, the house looked threatening. Like the river. Like the waterfall. It was not even the size of it, so much larger than she had expected. Nor the greyness. Nor the large, apparently curtainless, bleak windows. It was something else: the product of her own instinct. At that moment Jemima Shore felt the straightforward impulse to flee; to turn the wheel of the estate car and immediately go back. Back to civilization, away from Paradise and this island of Eden.

She recovered herself. Then she saw a tall grey figure, grey dress, grey hair, waving enthusiastically on the steps of the house. In its own way, that did nothing to encourage her. Not a ghost. An occupant.

'Someone lives here. I didn't know—' she began.

'No, no one,' he answered with surprise. 'Oh, that. That's Bridie. Only Bridie. She cleans for you. Cooks for you. Whatever you want.'

'Would she do nothing for me?' Jemima's voice, even to her own ears, sounded slightly neurotic. Colonel Henry shot her a look of amazement.

'Do nothing for you? Well, yes, I suppose so. She's always worked for us. Now she lives in the old Beauregard Lodge, the one we call the Black Lodge. Doesn't sleep in. Comes to work on a bicycle over the bridge.' He paused. 'Besides, she'll keep the Red Rose under control.'

It was said with a faint snort, not quite a laugh, still amused. It was the very first allusion he had made to the recent dramatic events in the church.

'It's just that I do so much need to be alone—' she began to sound like a hysterical child.

'She'll certainly keep away if you ask her. Ask her first, mind you. All the Stuarts are famous workers. She won't like doing nothing.'

'Stuarts—'

'Bridie Stuart. Born a Stuart on the Estate here and married Willie John Stuart from the west coast.'

'It's a common name round here, I suppose. No relation to—' She swallowed. She had nearly said—Captain Stuart. 'She's his mother, as a matter of fact,' answered Colonel Henry in his cheerful voice. His tone alone made it clear that Bridie was not a supporter of the Red Rose. But he added all the same:

'She doesn't hold with her son's weird ideas, naturally, any more than the rest of us do. Bridie's got a good head on her shoulders. I can assure you that the very last thing she would like to see is the Wild Island taken over by a lot of cranks, or whatever it was that my nephew had in mind.'

'Could you explain to me just what it is they want? Just for my own interest,' asked Jemima in her most tactful interrogator's manner.

'Utterly ridiculous,' was all Colonel Henry replied,

without deigning to explain what it was that was so utterly ridiculous. Then he relented: 'A Royal Memorial Island!' he exclaimed with another snort, giving the words ludicrous emphasis. 'In honour of the late and totally unlamented Bonnie Prince Charlie—of all people. Why, the fellow was a disaster for the Highlands in every way. No sense of military judgement whatsoever and finally left his own men in the lurch while he went off to France. Doesn't deserve all the attention given to him at Culloden, in my opinion, let alone another memorial up here in the Glen. At least my nephew's death put a stop to all that.'

'And now?' enquired Jemima in dulcet tones.

'Oh, these men calling themselves the Red Rose, Lachlan Stuart is just one of them, they actually want me to set up the Memorial Island all the same as a kind of Red Rose wasps' nest. With the house as a museum, as Charles had planned. Had the impudence to tell me that I ought to carry out my nephew's wishes. I sent them pretty sharply about their business, I can tell you. Told them I didn't want to hear any more about it. What with that and Father Flanagan: *he* thinks I ought to make the whole island over to his church, found a mission there... However, that's another story.' They had reached the house; the Colonel pulled on the hand-brake firmly. Then most courteously he helped Jemima out of the car. Bridie advanced down the steps. She was, even with her grey hair, handsome. Jemima could see the resemblance to her son. Unlike Captain Lachlan—when last seen—she was in fact smiling radiantly.

'Miss Shore, Miss Shore!' she cried. 'Welcome to Eilean Fas. And I was seeing you on the television last night. How clever you were. That terrible man and those terrible questions. And how pretty you looked—' She paused and looked extremely sharply and critically at Jemima. Her eyes, like her son's, were blue. They were extremely shrewd eyes.

'Aye, you look a wee bit older in the flesh. Mebbe it's the journey? Well, we'll soon feed you up, get some colour in the cheeks.'

'I think Miss Shore would probably like to be alone—' began Colonel Henry.

'Of course she would. You be off now, Colonel. I'll be looking after her.' There seemed no way of diminishing Bridie's enthusiasm.

'I'll just have a dram then,' said the Colonel. Jemima noticed it did not occur to him to ask her permission. 'Funerals, you know, an awful strain. What with my niece making an ass of herself. And young Lachlan. And having to shin up that dashed mountain when those absurd nincompoops tried to stop me from getting to the church. In my London shoes! What would Mr. Carter at Lobbs say? Still quite fit, you know. But the shoes were a bore.'

Jemima looked down at the once handsome shoes on his long narrow feet, scuffed and scratched; no wonder Ossian Lucas had refrained from joining the mountaineering expedition. 'Nothing like a little malt after a funeral,' ended the Colonel. 'And then I'll be off.'

'Of course. Do have a drink,' said Jemima sweetly. 'But I'm not sure if—my secretary sent a list—but I don't drink whisky.'

The conversation had distracted her from taking in the equally extraordinary nature of the interior of the house. There were antlers and heads galore, some tiny stuffed Disney-like faces, close at hand, some vast animals looming out at her from overhead; most of them accompanied by brass plaques stating when and where and by whom they had been shot. The hall itself was high and arched, probably the same date as the rest of the stone-built lodge, mid-nineteenth century at a guess. But there was an astonishing lack of furniture or even carpets in the hall, and in the rooms leading off it which she could glimpse through the heavy doors. Apart from the surfeit of taxidermy, old fishing rods in mouldering covers, a stringless tennis racket and what looked like a couple of croquet mallets constituted the main decoration of the hall.

'Oh, you have to drink whisky in the Highlands,' announced the Colonel airily. 'I'm sure Bridie's got something in her cupboard.' He led her into the dining room.

Bridie beamed. Jemima gazed at the same time at the tattered long curtains in the so-called dining room and at the sparse furniture—one large very stained wooded table and three chairs, two broken. If she had not been so firmly accompanied by Colonel Henry, she would have believed that she had stumbled on a forgotten house, some dwelling unaccountably deserted which had fallen into gradual ruin. But of course Tigh Fas was not deserted: she began to wonder helplessly whether she was ever, ever actually going to be alone since Colonel Henry was bound to stay on and on . . .

In the event she was wrong. Colonel Henry drained his dram very quickly, and speedily he was in the car again and away down the steep track.

'Come to dinner on Tuesday,' were his last words. 'Give you a few days to recover. Bridie will explain everything. She knows it all. No, you can't refuse. No telephone. One of my idiot sons will come to collect you. I should add that we've got the little Princess coming. Asked herself. But that needn't bother us.' He sprang into the driver's seat as though he was mounting a horse.

Bridie gazed admiringly after him. To her slight annoyance, Jemima found her own gaze was not totally untinged with feminine admiration. It must be the Scottish air—or even the very small deceptively pellucid dram of malt whisky she had been persuaded to taste. But she had felt first protected, then unprotected by the Colonel's disappearance. Come back for one moment, she longed to cry after him.

All her fears rushed back with his departure. The house no longer seemed welcoming. It had returned to its original sullen, rather sinister aspect. His voice no longer filled it. But at least she could be alone—once Bridie had gone.

In the meantime Bridie guided her gently into another large room where there was a fire. It was still rather cold. There were engravings of lochs and stags on the walls. The engravings were mottled with damp. The ancient patterned wallpaper, equally mottled, displayed an area of green and red and blue flowery undergrowth punctuated by birds, not unlike the vegetation she had noticed on her way up the island drive. There was still very little furniture, although the single sofa, like the dining-room table, was enormous. A bookcase with a glass front had lost two of its panes. The sparse collection of books inside, although distinctly Scottish in origin, did not look as if they would appeal either to Dr. Marigold Milton or Guthrie Carlyle.

'I'll be leaving you now for a wee while,' said Bridie gently. 'And then I'll be making your lunch.'

Jemima turned to protest. But she felt too tired. It had been a long time since that early-morning awakening in the sleeper outside Inverness Station.

At least she was alone.

She wondered what on earth had induced her to choose a Highland holiday, this northern Eden already proved so full of serpents. She had better enjoy her solitude while she could.

A few minutes later, or perhaps more, perhaps she had closed her eyes, there was a winching and cracking sound at the French windows which led to the grassy overgrown terrace. Someone entered.

'Well now, Miss Shore,' said the now familiar voice of Lachlan Stuart. 'And how did you enjoy the funeral?'

SEVEN

There's Tragedy Enough

'Look, I've brought you these,' said Lachlan Stuart. In his hands was a bunch of wild roses. Their colour was more pink than red. But the symbolism remained clear. Jemima felt herself to have conceived a hatred for all roses since her arrival in Scotland. In any case she had always hated red roses: a violent assault on the senses. She preferred bunches of white flowers: jonquils, narcissi in spring, with perhaps a touch of yellow permitted. White flowers suited the cool blues and pale greens of her flat overlooking the trees of Holland Park where Colette was now keeping watch. Spring flowers smelt actually erotic to Jemima. People who courted Jemima Shore quickly learnt not to send anything as crude as red roses.

In any case she decided she had had enough of Captain Lachlan and his problems: it was time to strike now if her whole holiday was not to be ruined.

'Mr. Stuart,' she said firmly in a voice which would

have been recognized at a programme planning meeting of Megalith Television, 'I have no wish to receive these flowers from you.'

'I have come to give you a message,' Lachlan continued, paying no attention to her interruption. His tone was oddly kind. 'These flowers are a message from the Red Rose. From our Chief. We bear you no ill will. We shall protect you. You will still be our witness. When the day of setting up the royal island comes.'

Jemima pretended not to understand the allusion.

'I don't need your protection,' she countered. 'I have no interest whatsoever in the contest you seem to be having with the Beauregard family.'

'But you must be interested in the Red Rose.' Lachlan sounded almost hurt. 'Seeing you're from the television. A reporter.' It seemed impossible at this stage to disillusion him sufficiently to explain the vast difference between the useful programmes of social comment and enquiry which Jemima Shore, Investigator, was wont to conduct, and the kind of reporter he evidently had in mind. Lachlan continued: 'Aye, but contest is the right word for it, you're correct about that. For you're knowing already about the Prince's island, I'm thinking.'

Jemima said nothing. She saw no reason to recount her brief conversation with Colonel Henry.

'The royal island,' said Lachlan impatiently. 'The Bonnie Prince Charlie Memorial. Here on the Wild Island. He told you, Mr. Charles. You were to witness the setting up of it. That's why he invited you here, where no tenant has been for years. It was all part of his plan, seeing you were from television. You would make a programme about it all, and the world would see that justice had been done to the memory of the rightful King of Scotland. He wrote to you—'

'I know very little about Bonnie Prince Charlie. And I

know still less about Mr. Beauregard's plans for setting up a memorial to him. He certainly mentioned none of this to me in his letter...' Even as Jemima spoke, she had a sudden vision of Charles Beauregard's last letter: that scrawled handwritten postscript, whose tone contrasted oddly with the rest of the businesslike formality, typed presumably by a secretary, since his original letter had been convivial, even rambling. 'PS. There is another matter concerning Eilean Fas which I should like to talk to you about personally. It can't be put in a letter.' No, indeed. If the late Charles Beauregard had really hoped for some sort of television special on his Memorial Island, he would have been sadly disappointed. She tried to imagine the reaction of the head of Megalith Television, Cy Fredericks, to her request: 'Cy, I've discovered these charming Scottish eccentrics—' 'Most exciting,' he would say. 'Most exciting. We must discuss it.' And then, without a pause. 'As we were saying about Northern Ireland...'

Now she merely repeated more firmly than ever to Lachlan: 'The troubles of the Beauregard family, their finances, and indeed the Red Rose itself I am afraid do not concern me. No one here seems to understand that I'm actually on holiday.' The slightly desperate tone of the last remark echoed in her ears. To combat it, she stepped forward defiantly, picked up the bunch of reddish roses from the cracked, barely polished wooden table and put them on the fire. A few petals fluttered onto the carpet, worn and hardly still colourful, as she did so. The petals lay between Jemima and the fire, like pale bloodstains, which someone had vainly tried to wash out. Neither Lachlan nor Jemima made any move to touch them.

'This is a lonely place for a woman, I'm thinking,' said the man after a long silence.

'I've never minded being lonely. In fact I've come here

to be lonely,' replied Jemima. It was true. She had never minded loneliness. Her solitary upbringing, the death of both parents when she was eighteen, her struggles, the life of a successful woman with an enviable career in London: would any of this have been possible if she had been temperamentally incapable of loneliness? Those years of her affair with Cy Fredericks, gay, hectic, tortured years of her late twenties, those later so much less gay years of her early thirties awaiting the call of the married MP, Tom Amyas... No, none of that would have been possible if she had been dominated by fear of loneliness.

Nowadays life was good. Guthrie Carlyle, if anyone, was the lonely one. But she certainly did not feel like sending for Guthrie: something about his evident willingness to be summoned at all hours of the day and night, at all seasons, so charming in a busy London life, had seemed to make his summoning unnecessary in the Highlands. Better far to beguile herself with his presentation copy of Burns, beside the fire, alone. Once, that is, Lachlan Stuart had been quickly but firmly eliminated.

'Aren't you afraid of ghosties, then?' There was something faintly mocking about Lachlan's voice. 'If you'll no be interested in royalty. Wummin is generally afraid of ghosties.'

Jemima smiled and said, 'I'm sorry to disappoint you.' In her experience, ghosts turned out to have an all too human explanation. Beware of charms, ghosts, dreams and such like fooleries said the Catholic catechism. As Mother Agnes would say. She thought of Blessed Eleanor's Convent. Ghosts were evil manifestations in her experience, but human evil not supernatural evil.

'This is an ancient place,' said Lachlan. 'And there are ghosts here, good ghosts. But you'll no avoid the ghosts at the Wild Island. That's a Druid ring yonder, they told us as boys. And Sighing Marjorie herself at the waterfall, you'll hear her voice yourself before long, above the noise of water, yearning, crying out, and other ghosts too, not so far away, ghosts they say from the wartime, the soldier killed at the falls, and now the ghost of Mr. Charles, his Majesty King Charles Edward, whose memory still calls out to us. This is a Wild Island, and there are things here you from the South will never ken, but these things will not leave you in peace, even if you be from the South. There'll never be peace here till the flag of the Red Rose flies over the island, and the memory of Bonnie Prince Charlie is laid at rest. That's why you'll need to be protected.'

A strange chanting note had entered Lachlan Stuart's voice, less like the mocking note when he had first entered the room, more like the keyed-up note of his words in the church: 'Her Majesty Queen Clementina.'

And all the time the noise of water, loud, rushing water, filled Jemima's head. And behind him through the French windows, curtainless except for some tattered chintz, with their cracked and splintered woodwork, arched another rainbow. Brightly it leapt out of the soft remorseless rain which would not surrender its fall even before the many hues of the prism. The noise of the water grew louder and louder in Jemima's ears. She began to have a strange fantasy that the river was rising, invading the house, covering the island . . .

She thought, 'I can't stay here, I shall never sleep here with the noise of that water.' Then Lachlan's face swam before her eyes. The rainbow splintered and its violent colours dazzled and enveloped her. She knew she was going to faint.

When Jemima opened her eyes again, she was sitting in the rubbed leather armchair next to the fireplace. Outside the windows the sun was shining, catching the currents of the black river with gold. It was a delightful prospect.

There was no rainbow. And no sign of Lachlan Stuart. She was quite alone.

The two whisky glasses had vanished. She began to believe that, exhausted, slightly drunk from the whisky on an empty stomach unused to it, she had imagined the last intrusion.

'The roses,' she thought. She looked down at the hearthrug. There were no petals to be seen. The fire itself was neatly banked with logs.

She had absolutely no idea of the time. Her little gold bracelet watch, a present from Cy—she had noticed something similar on the wrists of other bright girls at Megalith from time to time—said five o'clock. That was absurd. It must have stopped during the night. She put the delicate object to her ear. The sun was shining so disarmingly: evening could hardly have arrived.

'Aye, it's a beautiful evening we have to welcome you,' said a voice from the door. 'And I've brought you a nice tea. I'm sure you're ready for it.'

It was Bridie Stuart. She was carrying a large mahogany tray. On it were piled a series of plates containing biscuits, buns and combinations of biscuits and buns, as well as a sponge cake, evidently so freshly made that it gave the impression of still softly steaming. Within its layers were seductive glimpses of cream and jam. There was food enough on the tray for ten people.

For one horrified moment, still drugged with sleep, Jemima imagined that others might be expected—

'Och no, it's just that I looked in at lunchtime and you were fast asleep. Sleeping like a child. So, seeing you missed your nice lunch, I thought a wee cake, and some buns. With you being so thin.'

Bridie put down the tray. She was a strong woman, as well as a tall one. She carried the heavy tray without visible effort. Then she knelt down and poked the fire.

Questions thronged in Jemima's head. Who had rescued her from her fainting fit? Surely she had fallen onto the floor, and not thus neatly into a chair? Lachlan? His mother? Or both? She had no idea if Bridie was even aware of her son's visit.

'The flowers—' she began cautiously. 'Those red petals.'

Bridie looked round from the fire, positively beaming.

'I knew you'd like them,' she said with great satisfaction. 'I brought them from my little garden. Seeing as there are no flowers here at Eilean Fas.'

For the first time Jemima noticed a vase beside her. It contained a quantity of lurid but clearly home-grown roses. They were each of them a different shade of red.

'But the other petals on the hearthrug,' she persisted. 'You cleared them away?'

Bridie did not stop smiling. She dusted her apron and arose.

'Och, those flowers won't fall yet awhile,' she replied. 'Look, they're freshly picked. Not like your London flowers! Lady Edith tells me they're quite dreadful, scarcely bought but they're dead.'

'Your flowers are quite beautiful,' said Jemima hastily. She could not resist adding, 'Are you particularly fond of red roses?'

'I'm powerful fond of all flowers,' replied Bridie. 'It's just that red roses grow very strongly hereabouts. The white roses now, they won't thrive. Lady Edith Beauregard's beautiful garden, all the white roses she planted there, brought from the South from her brother's place—that's the Earl of Bournemouth, she was Lady Edith de Bourne before her marriage—' pointed out Bridie in parenthesis, in her kindly way—'and she's awful fond of flowers, flowers in every room, collecting wild flowers, making a garden. A real lady. Anyway they all died. In one night. It seems they were from the South and wouldn't grow in our Scottish soil. That's what Robbie, the gardener, said. And Mr. Charles, he had the famous white rose garden up at the Castle replanted with red roses.' She paused. 'No, all the roses you'll see growing in Glen Bronnack these days, Miss Shore, will be red.'

It was impossible to tell from her expression whether Bridie either approved or disapproved of the phenomenon: a valley where a white rose would not—or could not—grow.

'Now eat, Miss Shore,' said the older woman in a kindly voice. 'These things need not concern you, you with your tea to eat.'

Jemima gave herself up to the array of Bridie's confectionery, and discovered that she was quite astonishingly hungry. Bridie continued to stand over her, talking as Jemima ate. It was clearly a situation in which Bridie rejoiced: the visitor as the grateful devourer of her wares, herself as the expositor of the ways and doings of Glen Bronnack, narrowing onto the precise details of Eilean Fas itself, and the house Tigh Fas.

As Jemima ate four buns without difficulty, Bridie gave her a quick geographical sketch. She spoke of Kilbronnack House, 'residence of the Colonel and Lady Edith,' just outside Glen Bronnack and conveniently adjoining Kilbronnack itself.

Bridie spoke of the town too, which she described as a wonderful shopping centre, in every way superior to Inverness, and in some ways infinitely better than London, as Lady Edith herself had confirmed to Bridie. She then came to the subject of Eilean Fas, the need to be careful crossing the bridge at all times. And then she spoke of Tigh Fas, the sadness that the Estate had let the house run down, no curtains, no proper furniture, and how Jemima's unexpected appearance—'a tenant at Tigh Fas, I was awful delighted'—was thought by Bridie to herald a wonderful new era when the Estate would have to renovate the house again. She made no mention of the late Charles Beauregard's plan for a Bonnie Prince Charlie Memorial.

Finally she talked of the capricious ways of the Aga cooker which only Bridie could understand. She talked of food, food which she seemed anxious to cook for Jemima, and which she implied could be best obtained from Kilbronnack with her, Bridie's, approval, or at least connivance.

'You having no car,' said Bridie half hopefully, half accusingly. 'And the telephone not being here, it was never worth the bother, with the house so empty. And the nearest telephone being at my house, the Black Lodge that is.'

Jemima let the point go. From the South, how delightful a Paradise without telephone or car had seemed. That mood had temporarily vanished. Something about the house was still making her uneasy: the lack of telephone or transport did not help. She would have to arrange for a car at least. But she was not prepared to discuss the subject with Bridie.

'You're very kind,' she answered. 'But I shall just be camping here. I don't really eat much myself. Besides,' she attempted jocularity, 'your tea will last me for several days.'

'But you'll be having some visitors, now?' There was a new avidity in Bridie's voice. She pronounced the word visitors, as Colonel Beauregard had pronounced the word tenant—with a mixture of awe and something like lust.

'No visitors.' Then she compromised. 'I'm planning a new series of programmes for the spring. I need absolute quiet.'

The mention of hallowed television led to a temporary

lull in Bridie's offers; Jemima suspected it might, however, be no more than a truce.

In all this it was noticeable that one topic on which Bridie Stuart did not dwell was that of the late Charles Beauregard. Yet he had presumably been her employer—until his death. It had been made amply clear to Jemima that young Charles Beauregard, not the much older and maturer Colonel Henry, had been the owner of all this vast estate, these lodges, this castle, this house in which she found herself. Even Kilbronnack House, Bridie made it clear, belonged to the Beauregard Estates, not to 'the Colonel perrssonally' as she put it, rolling both the r and the s. It must have been an odd feeling for the Colonel and his lady not even to own their own home...

The omission of the name of Charles Beauregard was all the more noticeable in the case of Bridie, since she spoke at such loving length concerning her own charges, the vast, in every sense of the word, family of the Colonel and Lady Edith.

'Mr. Ben, aye, what a handsome lad he's grown into, he was my first baby, the flower of the flock said Lady Edith many times to me, and flower he is indeed... Mr. Rory then, he's much quieter of course; indeed he's awful quiet but verra charming when you know his ways, a deep one I called him as a baby, slow to walk, verra deep, but walking verra fast when he did learn with his long legs, and of course he loves it here so much. Ah sure it's a tragedy there's no work round here. But there's no work for him in the Glen, so he has to go away to get work, travelling so often, even to London. Many's the time he's told me: Bridie, I would do anything in the world to live here, maybe here right at Tigh Fas, after all it's empty, anything short of murder, he'd say with a laugh.'

As Bridie bustled on in her narrative to further descriptions of Hamish (slow both to read and to walk) and

Gavin and Niall (slow both to read and to talk and to walk, this time, so far as she could make out, and now following useful unmemorable careers in outposts of the former Empire or the Army), Jemima brooded on Bridie's last words concerning Rory. Was it Rory? Yes, Rory. She would never learn to tell them apart, and hoped she would never have to. But this was the second time today that a member of the Beauregard family was quoted as having spoken yearningly of murder. Death and land. 'A Glen worth killing for,' Colonel Henry had told Duncan. Rory had said of himself that he would do anything short of murder. What a primitive lot, thought Jemima with distaste. There was one thing of which she was quite positive: not all the land in the world was worth the sacrifice of a man's life.

But the line of Beauregards seemed like Banquo's descendants to stretch till the crack of doom.

'Isn't there quite a young boy as well?' she enquired.

'Aye, that's Kim,' said Bridie. Her voice was quite doting. 'My baby. He's fifteen.'

By now the tea, the gargantuan tea, had been despatched. Bridie took the tray. Jemima followed her into the hall to the ancient kitchen with its range, like something out of a deserted mediaeval hall. Even here there were antlers, heads, lesser heads, servant class. In the hall of the house she stopped beneath one gigantic head and read the plaque:

'Shot by Charles Edward Beauregard. Cwm Fair. September 27, 1930.'

For a moment the date baffled her, then she realized that the sportsman in question must have been Charles's father, Carlo. Another large plaque read: 'Shot equally by Charles Edward Beauregard and Henry Benedict Beauregard, October 2, 1932.'

'They never could agree who shot that stag,' said Bridie,

following the direction of her gaze. She was now attired in headscarf and mackintosh. 'So they had the plaque made for them both. What times we had here: when the house was gay, full of visitors.'

With a start Jemima realized that Bridie, for all her weather-beaten appearance, must in fact be about the same age as the brother Colonels. There had been a charming wistfulness, a youthful reminiscence in her voice, quite different from the doting maternal tone with which she had spoken of the Beauregard children she had nursed.

Outside Bridie wheeled an ancient bicycle from behind one of the thicker green shrubs. She was preparing— reluctantly—to go. Jemima herself decided to explore a little of the island while the light lasted. She had no wish for the woman to prolong her stay, still less to unleash another flood of reminiscence. Nevertheless the sight of that double plaque filled her with a sudden urge to ask at least one of the many unanswered questions which she felt still lay between her, as tenant of Tigh Fas, and Bridie Stuart, its imperial guardian.

'It must have been a great shock to you,' she said impulsively. 'I mean, the death of Mr. Charles Beauregard.'

Bridie, half on her bicycle, turned her face towards Jemima. The seamed face, till now so warmly creased, so jolly in the intensity of its recollected memories, was totally transformed. Gone was the friendly, garrulous, almost effusive woman, still essentially a servant. The woman who now faced her was a person of authority. And she was aware once more of Bridie's commanding height, standing by her battered bicycle as though a charger.

'Miss Shore, if you please,' she said after a moment's pause in a very flat voice, 'there are some things best not spoken of.'

Jemima felt a surge of determination. Her combative spirit was aroused. The flood of family reminiscences

Bridie had given her concerning the Beauregards contrasted so ill with this wall of sinister silence. She would have accepted one or the other, but not the ambivalence.

'I didn't mean to upset you, Bridie,' she said. 'But as I had corresponded with Mr. Beauregard—' She felt she might have added, 'and as I was forced to attend his funeral by your son, his existence and death can hardly be totally ignored.' In fact she said, 'I just wanted to express my regrets to you. Before walking round the island.'

Bridie said, with a return to her old and friendly manner, 'If it's round the island you'll be walking, Miss Shore, you'll best be wearing gumboots. It's wet underfoot here, even in the summer. And we've had a great deal of rain lately. It's slippery, you see, particularly at the far end of the island. Be very careful by the Fair Falls. Don't get too close to Marjorie's Pool, don't be curious—'

'Curious?' Jemima merely repeated the word.

'The pool where he drowned. Mr. Charles Beauregard; of whom you were speaking just now.'

Jemima was faintly appalled.

'Oh, how awful of me!' she exclaimed. 'I just had no idea he had drowned here at Eilean Fas. How clumsy of me—'

'Didn't the Colonel tell you then?' said Bridie in her previous flat slightly menacing tone. 'It was I who found him there in Marjorie's Pool. Lying face down. Drownded.' She gave the word two long syllables.

'Oh, how ghastly—and how terrible for you.'

'Yes. A terrible death. The water filling his waders, his great boots, to his thighs. Sucking him down,' replied Bridie without expression.

She was by now mounted on her bicycle. Over her shoulder she called: 'So be careful now, Miss Shore, won't you, as you go? We've had tragedy enough at Eilean Fas.'

Bridie was already riding vigorously down the gravel path, before Jemima realized that she had still expressed absolutely no regret concerning the death of the late Charles Beauregard.

EIGHT

Utmost quiet

'I must always remember this,' thought Jemima, as she set out to walk round the Wild Island. 'This at last is my Paradise. The serpent has come and gone.'

The evening sun began to create long blue shadows on her path, but it remained bright. The alternate patches of sun and shade gave a theatrical impression. The greenness of the undergrowth rustled with birds: she knew they were birds because every so often one flew out across her path, small, alien, not the sparrows of a London walk, darting purposefully.

'Birds of paradise,' she reflected. How long since she had heard bird song? Heard and listened to it. There were butterflies too. The Rousseauesque impression returned. She felt now neither loneliness nor fear. The ground squelched under gumboots she had borrowed from the house's antlered hall. They were much too large for her. Possibly everyone in Scotland had particularly large feet:

the other possibility was that no woman had ever lived in the house at Eilean Fas. The decorations certainly showed the lack of a woman's touch, to put it mildly, or rather they showed the lack of any recent touch at all. The house might have been deliberately gutted to make it seem so bleak. It was in a way no wonder that Charles had thought of it for a museum and Father Flanagan for a mission: it was bare enough for either purpose.

Above her head the vast trees rose out of the undergrowth: it was this which gave the jungle impression. Every now and then an opening in the trees exhibited a brief glimpse of the mountains round her: they too were lit up by patches of sunshine, out of their spare darkness, in the same theatrical manner as the trees. To the left, beyond the green, were the cliffs which guarded the island. In fact the path was in a sense treacherously close to the edge of the cliff, the greenery which masked it only enhancing the danger.

'I must watch my step,' she thought. The noisy river, ever present, should have served to remind her of the danger. But already the waters were fading in her immediate consciousness, no longer menacing, merely soothing. She had no idea where the path would take her, except she had been told by Bridie that it would take her eventually all round the island, so long as she did not turn off to the waterfall. At one end of the island, then, lay the domesticity of the house, the terraces now overgrown but symbolic of peace, the taming of the wild by man, the imposition of a human design, surviving much as relics of the Roman Empire survived into Ancient Britain. Even the view from Tigh Fas itself had an air of arrangement about it.

Now she was approaching a much more rugged terrain. The undergrowth began to encroach across the path. She no longer felt like some lady gently wandering in her domain, but more like an explorer.

A vista of bright red berries, heavily ornamenting a slender tree, entranced her, until it occurred to her that here at least was a hint of the future dark amidst the green present. One or two of the trees were already turning scarlet. It was after all getting on in August. Even a green paradise could not be guaranteed to last for ever.

Turning a corner, the sight of a little stone building of Gothic design, a kind of folly, at the edge of a clearing, took Jemima completely by surprise. Suddenly the trees had fallen back. She was at the point of the island. The noise of the waters had vastly increased: the waterfall and Marjorie's Pool must be close, but still unseen. The cliffs were now revealed to her, descending sheerly on either side of this sort of summer house, which had been built to perch precariously on the apex.

For the first time she understood clearly the impregnable nature of the island. The fall of cliff was steep, steeper surely than at the bridge, and looked precipitous, unfriendly. A few slender plants grew rather desperately out of the crumbly rock. But they offered little comfort to the potential climber.

Jemima decided to investigate the Gothic folly. Despite its little arched windows the interior was dark. It took her eyes some time to get used to it. No one appeared to have been inside for years. She took another step into the gloom and felt in front of her. Suddenly her fingers closed on something soft, familiar. Petals. And as her eyes grew accustomed to the interior she became aware that a vase of fresh roses, crimson, true roses, no wild roses, these, was standing on a plinth at the back of the grotto.

Jemima's shock was quite out of proportion to the situation, she decided a minute later. It was just that she had convinced herself of the utmost quiet, even isolation, of her new existence. 'Utmost quiet required for TV personality': so had begun the advertisement Cherry had placed in *The Times* with her usual desire for positive action.

'We've *got* to get Jemima to take a *break,*' Cherry was overheard telling Guthrie in the Megalith office. As usual Cherry managed to emphasize more than her fair share of words in each sentence.

'From the series—yes. After all she's not recording again till October. But from us all? I hope not.' Perhaps it was the sudden wistfulness in Guthrie's voice which irritated Jemima and inspired her to sweep into the outer office and immediately O.K. Cherry's somewhat over-dramatic advertisement, which had in its turn produced the original approach from Charles Beauregard. And now her utmost quiet was pierced once more by the manifest presence of another human being on the island.

Above the vase was a plaque, which read:

'In ever-loving and reverent and loyal memory of Charlotte Clementina Stuart, only legitimate daughter and heiress of King Charles III of Great Britain. Wife of Robert Beauregard of Kilbronnack. 1746–1764.' A rose was carved beneath the lettering, and beneath that the motto: FLOREAT ROSA ALBA.

There was a second plaque below which read:

'In ever-loving and reverent and loyal memory of Charles Edward Beauregard 1916–1944, lawful descendant and heir of the Royal House of Stuart. Placed here by his wife Leonie Beauregard *née* Fielding 1918–1958. FLOREAT ROSA ALBA'

Looking closely, Jemima decided that *Leonie Beauregard née Fielding*'s own dates had been added more recently.

She went back to the first plaque and puzzled over it: 'Only legitimate daughter and heiress of King Charles III...' Working it out, Jemima realized that King Charles III must be another name for Bonnie Prince Charlie, in legitimist terms. She remembered reading somewhere that there would be a problem when our own Prince Charles of the House of Windsor ascended the throne as Charles III, since loyal Jacobites would consider Bonnie Prince Charlie to have enjoyed that title already.

At least she was beginning to have a dim understanding of the nature of the Beauregard claim to the royal throne. Or rather the claim of the Red Rose on behalf of the Beauregards. They were descendants of some eighteenth-century royal ancestress. But—'Charlotte Clementina Stuart' —she felt sure she had never read about this particular character in the history books. Charlotte Clementina had apparently been born around the time of the rebellion of the '45, just after it, no, wait, the battle of Culloden was fought in April 1746, she remembered from her *Northern Guide*. Some time just before or after the collapse of Bonnie Prince Charlie's bold Highland effort, he was alleged to have produced this *legitimate* daughter . . . And heiress.

It was the legitimacy which baffled her. Who was the mother of Charlotte Clementina? Who was Bonnie Prince Charlie supposed to have married according to the history books, come to think of it? She would have to enquire.

Then here eye fell on a further notice—not chipped elegantly in stone this time, but written in ink on a piece of white paper in large flowing black handwriting.

'In ever-loving and reverent and loyal memory of Charles Edward Beauregard, rightful King of Scotland. 1945–1975. Placed here by his sister Clementina Beauregard. FLOREAT ROSA RUBRA.'

There was, as Lachlan had said, blood on the rose now: the Jacobite white rose of the first two memorials had turned to red. In case there was any doubt about it, scrawled at the bottom of the white paper was the single afterword: REVENGE!

Jemima felt a certain sense of relief. The flowers had been placed here by that poor distressed girl, with her obsession about the death of her brother. She had, in a sense, every right to penetrate the Wild Island. She doubted if her utmost quiet would after all be much disturbed now the flowers and the pathetic paper memorial were in place.

Jemima rose from her knees, dusted her beige trousers and left the grotto. She was determined now to visit the waterfall. Retracing her footsteps carefully from the point of the island, with wary glances at the chasms on either side—the grotto was built like a figurehead on the prow of the cliffs, it was a wonder it did not fall into the abyss—she returned as far as that mossy parting of the ways at which she had noted a left-hand path. The rise in the volume of water noise encouraged her. She pushed her way through the greenery: here was a path it was difficult to believe had been recently trodden. As if in sympathy with her desire to find water, the rain began its soft descent once more. Nevertheless the sun still gamely shone.

And it was by virtue of this combination that Jemima perceived the Fair Falls for the second time under the perfect arch of yet another rainbow. Only this time she saw the arch literally doubled: there was another rainbow described inside the first one. She was reminded of that line in the ballad: 'The old moon with the new moon in its arms.' Sir Patrick Spens—another Scottish hero who had gone at his King's command to Noroway over the foam. If not very near Dunfermline town, this was still ballad country. The foam and fine spray flew upwards in the air recklessly, as the black water poured down between the rocks into the chasm below. The pool was at a vast distance below her feet and the grass so slippery that she drew back nervously even before recalling Bridie's warning.

Could that dark and turbulent area of water really be Marjorie's Pool? Little as she knew about fishing, it seemed an odd place to choose to wade out. The pool must surely be too deep for any kind of wading, however high the boots. And in this case of course the boots had not been strong enough... 'Drownded. Sucked down into the waters.' Bridie's flat voice echoed in Jemima's ears. She tried to shut it out. There was, to distract her also, a high singing sound above the noise of the water, which she could not quite place.

The next moment her eyes were involuntarily drawn away from the pool towards the opposite bank. She was aware of a man in long dark clothes standing there quite still, staring at her. Surprise made her unsteady, she almost slipped and had to grasp a rather inadequate bush on the cliff's edge to steady herself. Recovering her balance, she half expected to see Lachlan Stuart once more. But it was Father Flanagan.

It was not that his expression was particularly sinister or even angry. Yet with his height, his white hair and his dark clothes, he did have the air of a kind of figure of vengeance, a ghost come back from another world to demand retribution. The evening light, the rain, the spray, the rainbow whose vanishing end hovered close to where he stood, all contributed to the phantom-like impression; or was he merely gazing covetously at the island which, according to Colonel Henry, he wanted for the Church?

Father Flanagan continued to stare at Jemima. Then he sketched a sort of wave. It might even have been the sign of the Cross. His lips moved, but the noise of the waterfall, the chasm between them, prevented her hearing his words. Then he turned on his heel and vanished among the rocks. Jemima gazed down the river to the narrow bridge to see if he was intending to pay her a visit. There was no sign of anyone on the bridge. She was safe from intrusion.

Jemima gazed once more into the depths of Marjorie's Pool, thought once more, despite herself, of Charles Beauregard pulled down into its depths as his great boots filled with water, and later found—floating—by the stern and unlamenting figure of Bridie.

No, she would cast out such thoughts. She would remember only the magic of the island, her own Prospero's isle. By an act of discipline, Jemima turned from the Fair Falls and retraced her steps along the mossy overgrown path. Then she wandered more slowly in the general direction of the house.

The undergrowth still rustled, but the birds were no longer flying so freely. The hour was approaching true dusk. Twenty minutes later Jemima found herself once more gazing at that strange Gothic dwelling calling itself Tigh Fas, the Empty House.

This time her feeling of threat, danger, dread was quite unmistakable. It was not the lush green hospitable island which threatened her and spoke of danger. Even the waterfall and Marjorie's Pool, for all its connotations, spoke of tragedy rather than of danger. Yet the house, which should have been her refuge from all this, filled her with foreboding.

'An ancient place,' Lachlan had said. Had some foul deed been perpetrated on the site of this house hundreds of years ago? Sighing Marjorie, who was she? And whose death did she lament—or was it perhaps her own? Jemima, while not believing in ghosts, was prepared, gingerly, to accept that deeds of violence from bygone times could leave behind their atmosphere of cruelty and destruction. Even the Druids' ring, she supposed, might bring some kind of atmosphere with it from ancient times. What she could not explain was why she, rational calm Jemima Shore, Investigator, in the words of her own television series, should feel personally threatened.

The island undergrowth spelt safety. The house stretched towards her and she longed to flee from it.

Briskly, Jemima decided that these thoughts could no longer be indulged. She marched back up the gravel path, ignored the dark uncurtained windows, pushed open the studded door into the vaulted hall and switched on the light.

The rest of the house was in darkness. Clearly no one had been here since she and Bridie had departed together. Everything was just as she had left it. The old fishing rods, shooting sticks and other strange pieces of tackle still mouldered in the hall.

She was certainly alone in the house.

Jemima, with a delicious and exhausted feeling of freedom, went into the decaying drawing room and built up the fire with logs. Then she went into the kitchen and scrambled some eggs, congratulating herself at having beaten off the proffered ministrations of Bridie Stuart. She discovered the wine ordered in advance by Cherry—a sort of Highland Beaujolais, it seemed, the best the grocer could provide. Into the eggs went some smoked salmon, another present from Guthrie. ('I know how much you love it, and the lairds up there keep it all for themselves. You won't be able to buy smoked salmon in Kilbronnack.')

Later, sitting by the fire, toying with the idea of beginning *Old Mortality*, she could not imagine greater cosiness nor happiness. It seemed indeed a pity to ruin contentment by beginning the Scott at quite this juncture. Bed and a detective story—Jemima read them by the dozen for relaxation—was probably the answer.

The bath ran with rich brown water, disconcerting at first, particularly when mixed with her favourite Mary

Chess Gardenia bath oil which made her London bathroom smell like a luxurious greenhouse. But in Scotland
the water was already softer than any oil could ever
achieve. In any case the mahogany fittings of the bathroom hardly suited such luxuries.

The bedroom was equally firmly Scottish, not to say
Spartan: the chintz curtains, blue and rose-patterned,
hung tattered in places, like those in the downstairs
rooms. There was a general dearth of furniture and
ornaments—the only picture consisted of a vast engraving
over the fireplace, depicting Bonnie Prince Charlie himself in a rousing scene at the battle of Preston.

Nevertheless the large bed with its mahogany headboard
was in itself extremely comfortable, because the mattress
sank so deeply in the centre as to positively enclose
Jemima within its warmth. There were also three stone
hot-water bottles, still-warm relics of Bridie's ministrations.

Jemima listened to the noise of the water running
outside. There was no moon, and the few other sounds of
the night did not disturb her.

She felt secure, happy.

Jemima picked up her detective story, entitled, she
noticed, A Scottish Tragedy, a sort of modern-dress version
of Macbeth, which she had chosen at Euston for its cover
of tartan and a dagger dripping with blood. At the time it
seemed appropriate enough. Jemima felt cosier than ever
as she skimmed, sleepily but still pleasantly, through the
first chapter.

She was just turning the page to chapter two when the
sound of someone coming stealthily up the stairs told
Jemima that she was not after all alone in the house.

NINE

From the South

The staircase creaked. She could not be mistaken. This was no ghost, no projection of the haunted imagination. Someone was coming up the stairs, someone who would shortly reach the head of the stairs, turn towards her bedroom, softly deliberately—

Jemima Shore felt quite literally paralysed with fright. She could not even stretch out one hand. At the same time she heard rather than felt, or so it seemed at the time, her heart thumping in time to the muffled steps. It would have been prudent to have leapt out of the huge blanketed bed, maybe even to lock the door—if there was a lock. Perhaps she should turn out the little bedside light in order to gain a certain advantage over her assailant. These thoughts went through her head while she continued to sit bolt upright in bed, frozen, the thin paper pages of *A Scottish Tragedy* still clenched between her rigid fingers.

No, she definitely could not move. All she could think was that she was alone in an empty house, with no help at all at hand, alone on a wild island, and just as she thought, This is ridiculous, I'll get the police, I'll dial 999, she remembered that there was no telephone.

It was at that moment that the intruder reached the top of the stairs. There was a hesitation, a silence, then the creaking moved in her direction. In gathering desperation Jemima listened to some new softly muted sounds outside her door: then a horrible thought struck her—there were two of them. A kind of greedy whispering consultation was going on just outside her door, she could not hear precisely what, but they were dividing her up, they were deciding what to do with her, she knew it, and soon they would burst open the door—

There was the sound of scuffling, low down. Quite suddenly Jemima realized that there was nothing human outside: in fact, the whispers were snufflings, there was some kind of animal outside her door. Unless it was a human being who whined and scrabbled, with sharp nails, and sniffed avidly beneath the ill-fitting door. The snuffling changed to a kind of whining. In her shaken state, that was such a ghastly thought, a human monster, a Beast come to find its Beauty, sitting up in bed in her pale satin nightdress, that she had to reject it, put it away. Yet equally the idea of a straightforward animal there outside the door, nervous as she felt, was scarcely reassuring. Jemima had a particular dread of bears who sometimes featured in her bad dreams. The image of a bear-like monster, a kind of vicious Caliban crawling out of the undergrowth of the island in search of its prey, was both persistent and repulsive.

In the meantime the snuffling and sharp, horribly determined scrabbling continued. It was just as Jemima had recovered her courage, and decided that she who would valiant be must at least confront her enemy, that two short deep barks settled the question of the monster's identity. She was thus half way out of bed already, genuinely cold now in the inadequate satin, when the feeble catch of the door finally gave before the animal's assaults.

At which point a labrador, large, beige and friendly, burst into the room. She recognized him. It was Jacobite. His strong tail wagged with continuous energy, his nose continued to snuffle, now at Jemima's bare feet. Then the labrador paused, raced to the tattered chintz curtains, sniffed, paused again, and came back to Jemima's feet. Finally with more energetic wags of his tail, the vast dog leapt onto the bed, lowered his head, transformed himself from a labrador into a circular pile of golden fur, and went to sleep.

Still too amazed for much thought, Jemima followed him back to the bed. She got among the warm blankets again. Her will sapped by a strong mixture of relief and surprise, she saw no reason not to follow the dog's example. Putting out the light, putting aside *A Scottish Tragedy* (she would not pick up that particular book again in a hurry), Jemima laid her head on the pillow. Jacobite had considerately chosen to make his nest at the bottom of the bed. The dog's heavy breathing, or light snoring, depending on your point of view, soothed rather than disturbed her. She had certainly never slept with a dog in her room before; the fastidious cat Colette maintained the privacy of her nights absolutely. In the background the noise of the river began to float away. An instant later, Jemima joined Jacobite in sleep.

When she awoke it was broad daylight. Bridie Stuart was standing over her with a heavy tray. Sleepy as she was, she could still discern a hunter's breakfast, porridge, oatcakes, eggs and bacon, and a few other items at whose nature, except that they were farinaceous, she could only guess. Jemima never ate breakfast.

She was about to murmur politely, 'Is there any orange juice?' (Cherry could never have forgotten to order that prime need), when she was interrupted by a vicious sound from the bottom of the bed. Startled, because she had completely forgotten the dog, Jemima saw that Jacobite was growling angrily and determinedly in the general direction of Bridie. The golden fur on his neck stood up in a ruff.

Bridie herself looked genuinely startled and even—for one instant—frightened. Then she looked very angry indeed.

'Ach, the wicked dog. The devil. How did she get in here, Miss Shore?'

'I really don't know. Late last night, I heard a noise—'

'Ach, the devil,' Bridie repeated. 'She's still looking for him. She won't give up. She'll never give up.'

'He was so friendly last night—'

'He?'

'He, she, Jacobite, the dog.' As if in confirmation, Jacobite snuffled again towards Jemima and even licked her hand. Then he looked towards Bridie and gave another menacing growl. The fur on his neck, which had temporarily subsided, rose again.

'That's no Jacobite,' repeated Bridie. Anger or fright or a combination of both made her sound quite scornful. 'Jacobite would'na come here in the middle of the night finding a loose window at the back like a thief. Jacobite stays at Kilbronnack House where he belongs, with his owner. He's a good dog, Jacobite is.'

'Then this is—'

'His own sister. From the same litter. But as different a one from the other as—' a pause '—Mr. Charles and Mr. Ben.' Jemima patted the dog's head. At the same time her fingers felt a collar and a tag. She twisted it round and discerned in highly ornamental letters: 'I belong to Charles Edward Beauregard of Beauregard Castle.' On the other side, it read: 'My name is Flora.' To Jemima the two dogs were absolutely identical.

Bridie had recovered from her fright and anger. She put down the loaded tray. The dog—Flora, as Jemima must learn to call her—gave another distinct growl.

'Why does she growl at you?' Jemima felt she had to ask. Dogs were becoming more of a mystery to her than ever. 'She must know you so well.'

'Aye, she does that,' said Bridie briefly. The smiling welcoming Bridie was not in evidence at all this morning; the dog's appearance had evidently shaken her more than she cared to admit. Of the two women, yesterday's warm enthusiastic help and today's figure of indignation and scarcely controlled outrage—or was it fear—Jemima wondered which was the real Bridie.

'She was so friendly to me, a total stranger—' began Jemima Shore, Investigator.

'Miss Shore,' said Bridie, 'it's no concern of yours, mebbe, since you're only here from the South, and a tenant, to enjoy our lovely glen. But I may as well tell you the truth. I was never able to abide Mr. Charles Beauregard. Nor his sister. Nor what went on up at the Castle. I did'na hold with his ways. I told them so, when they asked me to work there. Young people, yet they weren't as young people should be. Not like Mr. Ben and Mr. Rory and my boys—'

'And the dog *knew* this—' Jemima's voice was incredulous. She could easily believe in Bridie's disapproval of anything even remotely un-Scottish which might go on in beloved Glen Bronnack. Particularly so, since her loyalties were so clearly involved with the other branch of the family, Colonel Henry, Lady Edith, and Bridie's vast brood of former nurselings. But Flora, to have joined in the feud was clearly a dog of extra perception.

'She knew all right. And as I gazed on him in the water, and then thought how I should help him, poor drownded creature, past all human aid, she rushed at me, bit my skirts, tore at my hand. Look, it's not healed yet, the doctor gave me an injection—' Grimly Bridie held out one large, red hand on which there was a patchwork of sticking plaster.

'She thought it was I who did it. But it was not I,' Bridie's voice gathered passion. 'Not I who did it. I know who did it mebbe, though I'm not saying so, mind you, or mebbe I have my own ideas, but it was not I who did it.' Then Bridie began to shiver, as though at the vivid appalling memory.

'Bridie, who did kill Charles Beauregard?' The question sprang to her lips. Afterwards Jemima was never quite clear whether she had actually pronounced the words or not. For at that moment, the loud sharp hooting of a car's horn caused both women—Bridie in her white apron over a thick woollen cardigan and tweed skirt, Jemima still only in her shell-coloured satin—to turn their heads.

The hooting had an imperious quality.

'Ye never hear the cars arrive up at the island,' muttered Bridie. 'The river drowns the noise.' She turned and left the room. Jemima heard her heavy footsteps descending the stairs. A door banged. Now there were swift light footsteps coming up the stairs and a high female voice calling: 'Flora, Flora, good girl, Flora . . . Where are you?'

The labrador leapt off the bed barking, the wag of her tail swiping the milk jug sideways. There were joyful sounds of reunion and greetings in which 'Bad girl, *good* girl' seemed to alternate.

Finally, framed in the doorway, appeared the slight figure of Clementina Beauregard. In a Mexican blouse, thin, almost transparent, with a coloured shawl round her shoulders, a long patchwork skirt, various necklaces of beads, zodiacal signs and silver fishes hanging on chains, and with her long curling hair flowing everywhere, she presented a charming if slightly inappropriate sight for a Highland morning.

Clementina Beauregard advanced on Jemima with a smile which was so fixed as to give an impression of strain rather than genuine welcome. She was also carrying a half-smoked cigarette in one hand.

'Miss Shore,' she cried, 'I'm so terribly pleased to see you. You will help me, won't you? No, don't say you won't. I've got something most important I want you to do for me. I mean, you are Jemima Shore, Investigator, aren't you? I say, oatcakes.' Without a pause, this fairy-like creature, so thin and pale that she resembled Titania rather than something more substantial and human, began to demolish most of Jemima's hitherto untouched breakfast.

As Clementina rattled on, the timbre of her high clear bell-like voice recalled to Jemima's mind her denunciation in the church: 'Murderers . . . ' Her chatter darted to and fro in its random phrases, cries, appeals, expostulations, irrelevances, catchphrases, like a bird, and in vain Jemima tried to interrupt her. In despair she glanced at her leather travelling clock—a practical present from Tom Amyas.

Nine thirty. At lest she had slept like the dead. The phrase struck her suddenly as a sinister one. She was not dead. No wild animal had molested her, only a harmless dog looking rather touchingly for its dead master.

'Perhaps, after my breakfast,' said Jemima at last, pleadingly, to try and stem the flow. At which her fairy tormentor jumped up and cried in despair:

'But I've eaten all your breakfast! Horrors! And Bridie

wouldn't dream of cooking anything for me. Such a disapproving old thing. How Ben and the boys stuck her as a nanny, I can't think, except I suppose if you have Aunt Edith as a mother, anything is preferable. Calling Charles and me depraved! I'm sure she's far more depraved with all her jealousy and wanting everything for Ben all the time and hating us.' Clementina broke into slightly hysterical laughter.

Jemima smiled with more politeness than she felt. She had a terrible feeling that she knew exactly what Clementina Beauregard intended to ask of Jemima Shore, Investigator. Why was it that everyone expected television to present its performers with a kind of magic wand, which would enable them to solve problems insoluble to mere mortals? As far as Jemima was concerned, she was beginning to think that television *created* more problems than it solved, certainly at this hour of the morning.

She was thus not totally surprised to find herself being urgently enlisted by Clementina Beauregard to solve the murder of her brother Charles.

'I'll pay you, of course,' said the girl, tossing her fair hair confidently. She seemed to have less hysteria when discussing money than any other subject. 'I've never had any money before. Everything went to Charles of course, and even when Mummy died, despite her being American, she went and left all the money to Charles too, because that's what Daddy would have wanted. But now with Charles dead, I've got it all, the money, I mean, and I want revenge, that's what I want to spend the money on.' Her voice trembled on the word revenge.

'Yes,' she went on, more calmly and coldly, 'I'm a great heiress now. My mother was an only child whose father invented something ghastly to do with machines which everyone absolutely had to have. No other relations at all. Now Charles is dead, I've inherited the lot, yet I have now no land, not even a house to my name, all that goes to the male heir,' she invested the last two words with virulent contempt. 'In fact I can think of no better use for my money than to bring my uncle Henry Beauregard to justice. After that I'll just hand over what's left to the Red Rose, which Charles would have liked, and I'll go away. Besides if I die without children, which is extremely likely as far as I can see, then any money I don't succeed in spending has to go half to the local church and half to the next owner of the Beauregard Estates. Father Flanagan, that old horror, and Uncle Henry, or Ben, still worse! Can you imagine? No, I'll give it to the Red Rose, and then I'll just go away.'

There were tears in Clementina's eyes, of anger, perhaps, lamentation for her brother, or just passion.

Jemima replied in as measured terms as she could: 'First, Miss Beauregard, you must realize that I'm here from the South and what you're saying is all gibberish to me. Secondly, there is of course no question of my investigating the death of your brother. I'm a television reporter, not a detective. Lastly, there is no question of my accepting money for it.' She was aware, even as she spoke, that there was a certain weakness of logic about the way she phrased her denial. Clementina pounced on the fact.

'Forget the money,' she said quickly. 'I didn't mean to insult you. I'm sure you're very well paid indeed.' Yes, Jemima wryly reflected, I am at least very adequately paid; in that assumption at least about television, Clementina Beauregard is accurate. The girl went on: 'I've got this complex about my money. It's so terrible, you see: I've got this money now, pots and pots of it, and I can do whatever I want, have whatever I want in my lifetime, but how did I get it? Why, by the death of my brother Charles—the only person I've ever loved. And now I've no one to love, no one to spend it on—' The tears came again, and began to flow down her pale pretty cheeks.

Jemima felt overcome by a sudden rush of sympathy for this frail spirit, crushed by the recent death of her nearest and evidently dearest relative. And as for the laws of inheritance in these parts, Young Duncan's words in the car came back to her: it was enough to turn a girl's brain to lose her home and brother in one fell swoop, and all for the accident of birth which made her female. Jemima forgot the charm of Colonel Henry's manner, as a comparatively rare feminist indignation began to burn in her breast. Why should an uncle dispossess his niece in this manner?

'Tell me all about it,' she said kindly, in her best Jemima Shore manner, laying her hand on Clementina's thin fingers. The girl was genuinely shaking. 'Maybe the mere fact of my being from the South will let me bring a fresh eye to it all. You've been through a terrible experience: I can help you get it into proportion. If you tell me all about it, I expect I can reassure you that however tragic your brother's death, nothing criminal has taken place.' As Jemima spoke these soothing words, she noted that one part of her incorrigible brain was already toying with a major autumn programme on female inheritance in the modern world and/or the problems of a Highland feudal society or both . . . And this was supposed to be a holiday.

'First of all read this,' said Clementina, 'and then see if you can reassure me that nothing criminal has taken place. Lachlan Stuart got hold of it somehow.' She fished a piece of paper out of a loose bag of vaguely Middle Eastern origin which hung over her shoulder and pushed it towards Jemima across the denuded breakfast tray, lighting yet another cigarette immediately afterwards.

Jemima read:

'Ben. Urgent. I've just heard he'll be up at Marjorie's

Pool this afternoon. He's on to us. Do something before it's too late.' The signature was H.B.B.

'Henry Benedict Beauregard,' completed Clementina as Jemima handed it back. 'And that's unquestionably my uncle's handwriting.'

TEN

A Royal Link

'Now I'll explain to you what it's all about,' said Clementina Beauregard, twisting one of her many necklaces, so that the cabbalistic signs jangled. 'And then you'll help me. I know you will.'

Jemima said nothing. In any case it was difficult to interrupt the girl in her flow of rhetoric. But she felt rising within her a genuine determination, part born of sympathy, part—she had to admit it—of feminism, to help Clementina bring her brother's murderer to justice. After reading that note, she could scarcely reassure Clementina that nothing criminal had taken place.

It was essentially a tale of two brothers, that Clementina unfolded. Charles Edward—Carlo—and Henry Benedict Beauregard, born a year apart, brought up together totally from their earliest years, had unfortunately, said Clementina flatly, loathed each other. Far from being boon companions, Carlo and Henry were brothers and rivals.

And how cruelly the law of primogeniture worked to exacerbate the situation! Carlo born to inherit land, wealth, a castle, the Wild Island, the Glen itself, the fishing, the shooting, the moors, the mountains; Henry to live in Kilbronnack House by his brother's permission for the period of his lifetime and—if he was lucky, and Carlo did not want to do it himself—manage his estates.

'Can you imagine Uncle Henry accepting that for a minute?' cried Clementina bitterly. 'He always hated my father from the moment he was born.'

'You can hardly remember that,' pointed out Jemima mildly. 'By the time you were old enough to remember your father—'

'I don't *remember* my father at all,' exclaimed Clementina, in her hysterical voice. She was by now smoking frantically, wild drags and puffs, and filling every available saucer on the breakfast tray with random ash, followed from time to time by a stub. 'Don't you understand? My father was killed on D-Day. Charles and I were born over seven months later. Over seven months my uncle had to sit and wait. And wait. And watch my mother. And think—if it's a girl, I get the lot. How he used to pray in that little white church. Oh God, let it be a girl. Oh God, give me the Beauregard Estates. And Aunt Edith, she prayed harder still because she prays harder anyway. Besides, by that time, there was little Ben, and little Rory, and little Hamish on the way—'

'How ghastly for your mother!' Once again Jemima found herself identifying with the female in the situation. She could imagine no more ghoulish predicament than that of this young pregnant widow, waiting, waiting, for the birth of the posthumous child, and all the time watched over by her vulture of a brother-in-law.

'You know that I was born half an hour before Charles. And they didn't even know we were twins,' remarked

Clementina in her hard voice. 'Time enough for the doctor to ring up Uncle Henry and say—"It's a girl." And he said—"Thank God!" And Aunt Edith fell on her knees and began to recite some dismal prayer or other. And then'—with savage glee, the words were pronounced—'Charles was born, tiny, delicate, but a boy. And Aunt Edith had to get up off her knees again.'

Clementina's subsequent account of her childhood had nightmare overtones from Jemima's point of view. The idea of this isolated valley—no paradise in the difficult post-war years—occupied by a grieving widow, alien to the Highlands, but nevertheless feeling it her duty to live there for the sake of her children, and employing her own vast fortune to beautify and modernize her husband's houses and estates, out of respect to his memory. Yes, the window in St. Margaret's Church was a war memorial—commissioned by Leonie Beauregard in honour of her hero husband. Jemima had rightly observed the knights. There were actually two crusader figures swimming in the blues and greens of the glass: Leonie had not denied the surviving brother his place in the epic of Colonel Carlo's death.

In the meantime that surviving brother, Colonel Henry, was in the unenviable position of actually running these same estates from day to day, a task for which his American sister-in-law was scarcely fitted. While in Kilbronnack House, Lady Edith continued to give birth to a huge family of sons—six of them. These boys were all born if not to poverty at least to a chronic lack of money; in this and in every other way their lives contrasted totally with that of their first cousin Charles—'frail and pale like me—we are, I mean were, very alike.' The Beauregard boys were born with guns and rods in their hands and loved both sports: but all the shooting and fishing for miles around belonged in theory to their cousin Charles.

Jemima was reminded of the line in the Christmas

carol: moor and mountain, field and fountain, it all belonged to Charles Beauregard. All throughout their childhood, only one life stood between the junior branch of the Beauregard family and these far reaching and prized possessions, which they meantime watched their father control and administer.

'A situation made for murder, that's what someone once said as a kind of hateful joke, pointing at little Charles in his cradle, with Uncle Henry standing over him. My mother overheard them. Then she used to dress us up as the Princes of the Tower, in black velvet, with our fair hair, you know, the Millais picture—partly of course to tease poor Lady Edith who put all her boys in kilts; they slept in them as far as we could see. One day someone said to Mummy: "The Princes in the Tower, eh? Aren't you afraid of Henry doing a Richard III on Charles? He's so very much in control here." '

It occurred to Jemima that the late Leonie Beauregard, in repeating these stories to her daughter, had scarcely attempted to smooth over a delicate family situation.

'What did she think of him? What did your mother think of Colonel Henry?'

'She *hated* him,' stated Clementina in her most positive and passionate voice. 'She hated him because my father hated him, and later she hated him on her own account because he was bad and wicked, and she was right in everything she said, now he's a murderer.' The trembling began again, and the sobs.

A little cool voice inside Jemima's head said: Hadn't the lady perhaps protested a little too much? In Leonie Beauregard's lifetime, Colonel Henry had done nothing so much as dedicate his life to the service of the Beauregard Estates; in short, the service of his nephew. Whatever the jokes and implicit threats, Charles Beauregard had survived more or less healthily till the age of thirty.

It occurred to her that the circumstances must have been odd in another way up in Glen Bronnack; a young widow, a handsome man, married but his wife permanently pregnant, the widow and the brother-in-law thrust together . . . She wondered if Leonie Beauregard had always hated Colonel Henry quite so much. Half of her money had been left to the next owner of the Beauregard Estates if her own issue failed: whatever her hatred, she had not thought to alter her will.

One last question, trivial perhaps, raised itself in her mind.

'That film,' she said, 'about your father and your uncle—was that all a fake?'

'*Brother Raiders?* Fake from start to finish. Except of course for the battle bits. But utterly fake about them loving each other so much. Uncle Henry went and sold the film rights of his life in a typically disgusting way to pay for the boys' school fees—that was his story. Actually it was part of his mania for self-glorification. I told you, they hated each other. And when my father got the VC posthumously, and Uncle Henry only got the MC, he said: "Even in death, I'm still only Carlo's younger brother." Mummy told me that too.'

'I'll try to help you, Clementina,' said Jemima. 'At least to live with the tragedy of your brother's death. I can't promise anything more. I'll talk to Bridie for one thing: I've got a feeling she knows something more than she's telling about what happened down at the pool. In fact she dropped me a broad hint to that effect just as you arrived. And I'm dining at Kilbronnack next week, so I'll keep my ears open—'

'I know you are. Lachlan told me.'

'Oh.' Jemima was disconcerted. 'I must say I had not quite reckoned with the excellent intelligence service of the Red Rose. I congratulate you.'

'Lachlan has a very good contact somewhere,' said Clementina vaguely. For a moment her vagueness sounded studied. Then she went on, 'All the people round here, I mean the *real* people, support the Red Rose madly. I mean, wouldn't you, against the lairds? They want a better deal, so they support the Red Rose and a new monarchy and an independent Scotland.'

'They may get that anyway,' pointed out Jemima. 'Red oil rather than the Red Rose. Do they really want a new monarchy, I wonder? I mean, would you seriously like to be Queen of Scotland?'

Clementina smiled for the first time openly and naturally, with great charm. She sprang up, still smiling, stubbing out her last cigarette, her necklaces jangling.

'Like it? I'd adore it! I'd do anything to make it happen. Queen Clementina the First. *Groovy*.'

It was on that note, which Jemima half-hoped was joking and half-feared was serious, that their interview ended.

That afternoon Jemima settled down in the empty drawing room, the grassy terraces falling away before her eyes to the river. It was raining again. But now there was no sun and thus no rainbow. Jemima wrote two letters, one extremely short and one extremely long. The short one was to Guthrie Carlyle: 'Darling, Just to say that I'm sitting here thinking about you, because I'm about to start reading *Old Mortality*. Love J.' She added a heart, her trademark. As she sealed the envelope, she thought: That's not even true. Actually I'm sitting here thinking about Colonel Henry Beauregard and whether that handsome distinguished-looking man could possibly be a murderer.

The long letter was written to the person whose opinion Jemima most respected in this world. She was also someone who, Jemima felt, kept her in touch with opinion in the next (if indeed it existed). Not only did she owe her

friend, Reverend Mother Agnes of the Convent of the
Blessed Eleanor, a letter but she desperately needed the
nun's lucid impartial view of the world of Glen Bronnack.
It was always a relief to marshal events for the consump-
tion of Mother Agnes. Since the strange Gothic events
which had brought them together a few years back,
Jemima had come to use Mother Agnes as a kind of
extra-worldly consultant. Several times the nun had managed to point exactly the right path for her own television
career, and all by a chance reflection in one of her letters.
Goodness, Jemima supposed, meant strength. But goodness being all too often its own reward, it was satisfying
how the goodness—or rather the good advice—of Mother
Agnes had enabled her, Jemima, to outwit Cy Fredericks
over her last contract: 'I am reminded of the parable of the
Unjust Steward,' the nun's letter on the subject had
begun, 'so often misunderstood . . . '

My dear Mother Agnes [Jemima wrote], I find myself in
a very odd situation here. It's not exactly working out as
the tranquil away-from-it-all holiday I outlined to you in
my last letter. What was that warning phrase of yours
about peace being an uncertain commodity in this world?
And how primitive communities had a habit of being prey
to primitive emotions. I've got a number of questions to
put to you, and would like your considered opinion, taking
into account the full teaching of Mother Church, as to
whether a house can have an evil atmosphere. But I'd
better begin at the beginning. In a way it's a tale of two
brothers . . .

Over the next few days the island at least recovered its
atmosphere of Paradise. Other than Bridie Stuart, Jemima
saw no one.

She visited the shrine again. The roses had died and
had not been replaced. But the sight of the shrine, and
the three plaques, two engraved, one handwritten, reminded

her that she had not yet ironed out the exact nature of the Beauregard royal claim. The Historical Introduction to the *Northern Guide*, beyond providing the information that Bonnie Prince Charlie had married Princess Louise of Something or Other in 1772 and had had no legitimate descendants, that royal line dying out in 1807 with his brother Cardinal Henry Benedict of York, was not much help.

The Prince's only recorded illegitimate offspring, a daughter, belonged to the period of his European wanderings, long after Culloden; she had been educated at a convent in France, and ended up as Duchess of Albany. All this threw no light whatsoever on Charlotte Clementina, born in Scotland just before or after the Battle of Culloden, and wife of Robert Beauregard of Kilbronnack. Nor did it establish who her mother might have been.

Jemima decided to swallow her pride and ask Bridie, although she dreaded the flood of family information which might follow.

She was wrong. Bridie merely smiled, faintly sarcastically; she then made some slighting reference to the nonsense talked by the Red Rose—and the late Mr. Charles Beauregard—but added:

'You'd best read the American book. It's all in the book, they tell me. I never read it messell, I've no time for such things. It's my pairsonal opinion that we've a very good Queen on the throne and no need for another one. But coming from the television, you'd be interested in such things.'

The next day Bridie silently handed her a privately printed red leather volume with a gold coat of arms stamped on it. *A Royal Link* by Leonie Fielding Ney Beauregard. So it was the author, not the book itself, who was American.

Leonie Beauregard's style certainly owed something to

her native land with its enthusiasm and colourful appreciation of all things Scottish. Nevertheless the facts, such as they were, emerged clearly enough from her narrative. The mother of Charlotte Clementina was named Marjorie Stuart, the daughter and heiress of the then owner of Eilean Fas. Purely local legend had always glorified Marjorie for the major part she had played in saving the Prince after the horrifying fiasco of Culloden. Around Kilbronnack they tended to feel that the role of Marjorie Stuart had been too much neglected, that of Flora Macdonald too much cried up in the official saga of the Prince's escape. Flora Macdonald might have behaved very bravely on the west coast. But on the east coast, immediately after Culloden, when the Prince's forces were routed, and he himself transformed from a prince into a fugitive, it was the lively and courageous Marjorie who had been largely responsible for his early getaway. As the legend had it, it was on Eilean Fas, secure in the secret depths of Glen Bronnack from the searching red-coated soldiers, that the young pair had lain out together. They were to all intents and purposes alone, Marjorie's father having fallen in the battle, and the property having passed to his daughter.

Fortunately or unfortunately, depending on your point of view, Marjorie was both prettier and more yielding than Flora Macdonald. According to tradition again, when the Prince finally got away to the west coast he left Marjorie behind with a permanent royal souvenir in the shape of his unborn child. But it was generally believed that both mother and child had subsequently died cruelly at the hands of the English soldiers: the baby first thrown into the pool beneath the Fair Falls, and the mother, jumping in to save her child, drowning in her turn. Hence the name of Sighing Marjorie: it was no wonder, after such a grim tale, that her phantom haunted the pool.

But it was here that the Glen Bronnack version as

related by Leonie Beauregard in *A Royal Link* deviated from the accepted story. In the Glen it was said that the baby had not in fact been drowned but miraculously survived her experiences in the water. Like an infant Moses, she had been rescued by her loyal Stuart relations and baptized Charlotte Clementina, brought up among them as a supposed orphan. At the age of seventeen she married Robert Beauregard of Kilbronnack, dying a year later giving birth to a son. From this marriage the present-day family of Beauregards were directly descended, the blood of Bonnie Prince Charlie coursing through their veins together with that of a sound but otherwise undistinguished Scottish family.

Furthermore, and here was the delicious crux of the matter, by digging about further into old tales and legends and traditions handed down from generation to generation by word of mouth, the enthusiastic author had reason to suggest that the Prince had actually *married* Marjorie Stuart in secret when he discovered her to be pregnant. 'Is it fanciful to suppose that our brave Prince and our courageous Marjorie thus planned to safeguard the royal Stuart descent, should he be captured and executed by the English . . . ?' enquired Leonie Beauregard boldly.

So there it was. A royal pedigree—of sorts—for the Beauregards.

After finishing the book, Jemima contemplated leaving her own offering at the shrine, some of the yellow bog plants she had found on the island. She decided that it would be a sentimental gesture. She was no American romantic. Besides, she was only a tenant. She did not want to be permanently possessed by the island or its history, nor indeed the Beauregard family and its feuds. She was a bird of passage. In particular she did not want to be possessed by the house, Tigh Fas.

She read *Old Mortality*—the good Scott—alternating

with Burns. On her walks at least, she felt a new balm being applied to her spirit. Warming towards Guthrie (because he had once suggested it) she even began to contemplate some kind of Highland retreat of her own, a cottage of course, a real cottage this time; it might even mean marrying Guthrie, but that too might not be an utterly impossible venture. Guthrie was in love with her, an attractive lover *and* unmarried, a rare combination indeed. It was certainly an ideal combination in Guthrie's own opinion: he sometimes appeared quite disconcerted when Jemima rejected the occasional proposal with which he punctuated an otherwise exceptionally easy and loving relationship.

'I can't think why you *won't* marry me,' he would say. 'Millions would . . . ' He was only half joking. There was of course the question of freedom. But no freedom lasted for ever and Jemima had enjoyed great freedom. Yes, she was beginning to feel very warmly towards Guthrie in her Highland Paradise.

In a way the prospect of dinner at Kilbronnack House was a tiresome interruption of this personal reverie.

The island was particularly peaceful that afternoon. The occasional small plump bird strutted on the terrace. Bridie, who had threatened to return to make her tea, despite Jemima's protests (she still could not accept this strange tenant's proclaimed self-sufficiency), did not in fact reappear.

Jemima changed into a long dark green jersey dress, elegant, discreetly sexy (she hoped): Jean Muir, a designer in whose clothes she always felt she could face the unknown. She awaited the arrival of whichever Beauregard would drive her to dinner at Kilbronnack House. Her escort was late. Perversely, this had the effect of making anticipation grow. She had succeeded in banishing Colonel Henry from her mind for the time being in favour of Guthrie and the possible future they might have together.

Now, as she waited, she found herself hoping that the Colonel had not forgotten his invitation. As she put it to herself, quite apart from anything else, she had a mission to perform for Clementina Beauregard.

When the car finally scrunched on the gravel, the river noise masking its approach, it seemed to come to rest with an extravagant squeal of brakes. She suspected a very young man must be at the wheel.

The man who burst in through the door a moment later was young, if not very young. He was wearing a kilt, topped by a black jacket, and looked at first sight the pattern of a romantic Highland figure.

But his opening words were in no way romantic:

'Miss Shore, I'm Ben Beauregard, something absolutely ghastly has happened.' It was all said in a rush. Ben Beauregard's face, with its full mouth and wide-set eyes, was twitching as he spoke, twitching uncontrollably. His eyes still met hers as he went on: 'It's Bridie. I've just found her body. In the river among the weeds, all tangled up with her bicycle. She must have fallen off the bridge. Miss Shore, she's dead. Bridie's dead.'

Before Jemima's horrified gaze, his features began to break up further. Finally, putting his face in his hands, Ben Beauregard began to sob, the harsh painful sobs of someone who has not perhaps wept since childhood.

ELEVEN

Is She Safe?

After a time the sobs stopped. When Ben Beauregard had regained control of himself, he said, 'Sorry about that. The shock, you understand. She was our nanny, we all adored her. The bridge *is* very slippery in the rain, we all used to tease her about her bicycle, it was so ancient, and how unsteady she was on it. She must have tumbled in. Then of course she couldn't swim: we used to tease her about that too when we went over to the seaside. Poor old Bridie.'

His words faded away. Quite a different expression crossed his face, verging on anger, or perhaps irritation was the correct word.

'Oh God, whatever's going to happen now? The royal visit. We've got Hurricane Sophie coming to dinner at Kilbronnack.' The contrast between his genuine feeling at the old woman's death and his laird-like exasperation at the inconvenience to his plans was almost ludicrous.

And when an hour later Jemima Shore found herself sitting in the drawing room of Kilbronnack House, she was still torn between admiration for Ben Beauregard's cool, and suspicion that he was fundamentally able to carry off such a distressing situation with such verve.

Ben Beauregard was certainly an efficient organizer, like his father. Somehow estate workers were conjured up out of the Glen, including Young Duncan, who lived on a croft just beyond Bridie's lodge. Jemima herself was driven directly on to Kilbronnack by Duncan, while Ben stayed behind to 'clear up a few details here' as he put it—which presumably meant dealing with the body and all the other paraphernalia to do with sudden and accidental death.

The last thing Jemima heard Ben say to his aides was: 'Lachlan. We must let him know.'

'There was 'na much love lost between those two,' answered an older worker dourly, one of those who had escorted Colonel Henry at the church.

'They were still mother and son,' was Ben's reply. He spoke with authority. His voice momentarily resembled that of his father. The men exchanged looks. Nobody made any immediate suggestion as to how to contact Lachlan. As Jemima was driven away, she reflected that the intelligence service of the Red Rose was so good that the news of the tragedy would probably reach Lachlan long before Ben Beauregard's official message got through. She decided to say nothing. It was Duncan, tragedy not having diminished his enthusiasm for reckless driving or conversation, who broke the silence.

'Aye, it was the dog that did it,' he observed. 'It was the dog knocked puir Bridie Stuart from the bridge. She couldn't forgive her for the death of Mr. Charles.' There was a horrible kind of relish in his voice: it was as though he was enjoying the excitement of it all. Perhaps if you lived long enough in a remote valley, it was more exciting than distressing when your nearest neighbour fell off a bridge and drowned? Or was pushed off a bridge?

'Flora?' enquired Jemima in a startled voice.

'Aye, Flora. I was seeing her by and by, bounding down towards Eilean Fas, just there by the bridge, looking for Bridie Stuart she was. And she so clever, knowing how the bridge was slippery, and Bridie going to make your tea, and it was there she would be able to upset her. Aye, Flora has more intelligence in her paws than most humans in these parts have in their heads.'

It was a nasty picture that his words conjured up. Jemima tried to drive it from her mind. Still, it was strange that the dog should have been sighted near the bridge that very afternoon, in view of her manifest hostility to Bridie. Unless of course she had been in attendance on Clementina: but Duncan had spoken as though the dog was alone. She decided not to encourage Duncan's conversation on the morbid subject further.

Nevertheless it was impossible to dismiss altogether the sinister image of the malevolent animal bent on drowning its prey. And when she arrived at Kilbronnack House, it was recalled to her by the sight of Jacobite. Admittedly the Kilbronnack dog was lying fast asleep by the log fire. He did not even acknowledge Jemima's entrance by a wag of his tail. At the same time, Jemima decided to give him a wide berth: she did not think she would easily learn to trust dogs again.

The welcome of Colonel Henry Beauregard was on the other hand a masterpiece of active charm and implicit tact. He managed by a diplomatic remark both to convey his distress over Bridie—'Forty years with our family'—and to dispose of the subject: 'We mustn't worry our little Princess about all this, must we? We want her to have a good time in the Highlands.' He cut an astonishing figure in his kilt, black jacket with silver buttons, and silver-buckled shoes: having reluctantly admired his figure and bearing in his London suit, Jemima now came to the equally reluctant conclusion that in Highland dress Colonel Henry Beauregard was one of the best-looking men she had ever seen in her life. Perhaps it was the effect of the kilt . . . Yet the Colonel successfully put in the shade not only all those of his sons present (kilted themselves) but even the image of the more dashing black-haired Ben, by far the best-looking of the sons. Perhaps Highland lairds, like Scottish whisky, improved with age?

She tried to distinguish the names of the other Beauregards present: three, the remainder having departed after the funeral of their cousin. Rory seemed pleasant enough, with nice regular features and thick brown hair. Hamish's kilt and sporran both looked rather long to Jemima's inexpert eye. That gave a stolid impression. The boy Kim, whom she had noted in the chapel, looked bright. But he was clearly in a great state of tension, probably over Bridie's death. He was in fact engaged in an argument with his mother, which only ceased when Jemima came near the group.

'Hush, darling,' murmured Lady Edith, but in vain. Kim continued to press his argument, whatever it was. Jemima recognized both the other male guests. One was Ossian Lucas MP, who waved his hand languidly in her direction. He was wearing a tight-fitting suit made entirely of some improbable tartan; frills exuded from his sleeves, and torrented out at his neck. His strong face topping the bizarre costume provided a remarkable contrast. The other male guest was Father Flanagan. The tall priest was lecturing—or perhaps hectoring would be a more accurate description—Ossian Lucas on the various failings of those people who were at one swoop Lucas's constituents and Father Flanagan's parishioners. He had angrily refused a drink, which might have softened his mood. 'I tell you, I'm consulting the bishop as to whether it may not be an actual sin to belong to the Red Rose,' Jemima heard him say earnestly.

'With no employment hereabouts, and those great big wages up at the rigs for the Southerners, you can hardly blame them if they turn to the Red Rose,' observed Ossian Lucas; but he sounded fairly indifferent to the problem.

Jemima was surprised that a Catholic priest should be asked to dinner to meet Protestant royalty: and the more so when there turned out to be an extra man at dinner. It transpired that Lady Edith had rushed over in a panic to fetch him, on hearing that Princess Sophie was bringing her lady-in-waiting to dinner, Father Flanagan being the only conceivable extra man available at short notice around Kilbronnack. At which point Kim announced that he too had been promised to come to dinner to meet the Princess, 'ages ago, you *promised*, Mum, so long as I wore my jabot.' Having got into his jabot he was not inclined to surrender his place at dinner. As Lady Edith was clearly much too weak to insist on his withdrawal—to the evident disgust of his brothers—they had to make do with an extra man at the table. As Rory said *sotto voce*, 'Mum always makes things worse when she tries to straighten them out.'

There was further trouble with Kim when Rory suddenly grabbed a glass out of his hand, sipped at it, and put it down with a highly disapproving expression. Whatever the boy was drinking, it was obviously not in accordance with the older brother's notion of what was suitable for his junior.

Touched by her hostess's discomposure, which was hardly surprising in view of the closeness she must have established with Bridie in the past, Jemima listened patiently to the stream of inconsequential questions Lady Edith asked her about television. Which was more than Lady Edith herself did: she asked the same question three times: 'Don't you find it very difficult about clothes?' In vain Jemima tried to give her stock answers to this particular stock question:

'I try to wear very simple things which won't distract the viewer . . . ' Like Jesting Pilate, Lady Edith did not stay for the answer, but always darted away and was found fussing in another corner of the drawing room, now straightening Kim's jabot, now bending down to dust Rory's shoes with her handkerchief.

'The dress you're wearing tonight certainly distracts the viewer.' It was Colonel Henry handing her a glass of champagne. To her surprise Jemima found herself blushing, something she was sure she had not done for many a year. To cover her embarrassment she admired Kilbronnack House, the beauty of whose classically plain early eighteenth-century façade had struck her on arrival.

The plainness of the exterior of Kilbronnack House was matched by the extreme plainness of the décor. In fact the large room was decorated more by people than anything else. There were a few dark oil paintings of forebears—kilted—on the walls. Over the fireplace, surveying Jacobite's sleeping head, was an inferior copy of the best-known portrait of Bonnie Prince Charlie.

'Our distinguished ancestor,' observed the Colonel with a quizzical smile, following the direction of her eyes. 'What nonsense all of that is! The Red Rose, I mean, pretending we're the real kings of Scotland. Damned unsuitable topic to discuss, just as Princess Sophie is about to bob up. But I must say I've no patience with all that rubbish. Of course when my idiotic nephew Charles took up with it—purely to madden me—every lunatic, dead-beat and drop-out on the Estate followed him. And as far as I'm concerned that's the whole story of this blasted

Scottish Nationalism in a nutshell. People who just want to stir up trouble. Came across them in the war: knew the type. Quickly got them out of the regiment, just as fast as I could. Don't want to go into battle with people like that.'

Jemima looked up at the portrait of the Prince. There was a resemblance somewhere . . . the pale youthful face surrounded by its tumbling hair. It teased her. Why yes, it must be Clementina Beauregard. So no doubt there was royal Stuart blood to some degree in the Beauregard's veins, even if the Colonel was right and it was conceived on the wrong side of the blanket.

They were interrupted by the arrival of the Princess. From the flurry and commotion outside Jemima imagined that the local constabulary were in attendance in force. The small figure who entered, escorted by Ben Beauregard, was for a moment an anticlimax. But Princess Sophie was dressed in brilliant red—her favourite colour, according to the press—and upheld by platform shoes to match. And even without her eye-catching dress, she would have commanded attention. Pop-eyed, fair-haired, a true Hanoverian in her looks, and not even a particularly pretty one, she nevertheless radiated confidence and, as a result, her particular brand of charm.

Hurricane Sophie she was to the press, her vitality having earned her the nickname. Strong men in the gossip trade had wilted away trying to keep up with the pace of her social life; 'does she never go to bed?' they had been heard to groan. Indeed it was all very unsatisfying from the scandalmonger's point of view, for when the young Princess did go to bed, it might be 6 am more often than not, but she was invariably alone.

That same vitality made her now the automatic centre of attention in a way Jemima suspected would always have been so, royal birth or no royal birth. Princess Sophie also had excellent manners. She was quite delightful to Lady Edith, instantly admiring the flower arrangements, whose beauty and choice Jemima had only just begun to notice. From Lady Edith's obvious pleasure, Jemima concluded she had arranged them herself.

To Jemima, the Princess expressed the most knowledgeable appreciation of her recent series:

'Actually, whatever the press says,' she added disarmingly, 'I spend most of my evenings sitting at home at Cumberland Place, watching television.'

'Yes, Ma'am, that's perfectly true. But with twenty-five people sitting round you watching as well.' It was one of the middle Beauregard boys.

The Princess, not in the slightest bit put out, pealed with laughter.

'Rory, don't give me away,' she cried. 'I'm trying so hard to make a good impression on Miss Shore. I'm her fan.' Princess Sophie rolled her round blue eyes flirtatiously in Jemima's direction, then in that of Rory Beauregard. Jemima was surprised to notice that within the bounds of good manners, this flirtation was kept up all the evening. She would have expected Ben Beauregard, so very much better looking, to have been the focus of the Princess's attentions.

Perhaps there was more to Rory Beauregard than met the eye. What had poor Bridie said about this particular nurseling? His deep love of Scotland and things Scottish: 'A deep one,' she had said. Perhaps it was this quiet strength which appealed to such a volatile character as Hurricane Sophie. And wasn't it Rory who had once told Bridie he would do anything in the world to live in the Glen? A whole series of declarations came back to her. Clementina: 'I'd do anything to be Queen.' Colonel Henry and the Glen: 'A land worth killing for.'

Her Highland Paradise had not after all cast out the

serpent. The snake still lurked, the serpent of covetousness, the primitive passion for land: land, wealth and position. Could it ever be eradicated? One had to realize that while Charles's death had made Ben heir to the Estate, Rory Beauregard was still in the position of a second son to Ben.

The evening itself was rather jolly. It was Colonel Henry, not Princess Sophie, who put an end to it. Regardless of protocol (to a background noise of Lady Edith protesting, 'Henry, you really can't, Henry, please'—'Can't I, my dear? Just watch me'), the Colonel said firmly at eleven o'clock: 'Now, Ma'am, we all know you've got to be up at six and open that dam on the west coast. We mustn't take advantage of your good nature and keep you up.'

Princess Sophie took her dismissal gamely, remaining flirtatious to the last: 'Oh, Colonel Henry, I believe you're trying to get rid of me—'

'Ma'am!' exclaimed the Colonel in gallant horror.

'Oh, I'm so frightened of the Red Rose on the way home,' went on Princess Sophie artlessly. 'You know they've told the press they're going to kidnap me while I'm up here. It was headlined in the *Express*: IS SHE SAFE? So horrid for one to read with one's breakfast.' She did not look at all frightened.

It was true that the *Daily Express* had led off that morning with a tumultuous denunciation of the Princess's security arrangements while in the Highlands, based on the notorious reputation of the Red Rose in those parts. They were acting, they said, on a tip-off received from an undercover agent who had daringly succeeded in penetrating this extremist organization. To most of their readers, Jemima suspected, and possibly to the *Express* itself, the news of the Princess's danger and the very existence of the Red Rose had arrived at one and the same moment.

'Such an unfortunate royal title, Duke of Cumberland,' the Princess added. 'Papa should never have been landed with it. I mean, he *adored* the Highlands, but knew no history at all so he could never understand why he was always hissed whenever he got out of his sleeper at Inverness. If I was Princess Sophie of Surrey, no one would pay me any attention at all.'

'How many police—' began Ossian Lucas.

'So I thought Ben and Rory and Hamish would come with me back to the Railway Hotel,' continued Princess Sophie, 'and beat off the Red Rose. You too, Mr. Lucas, you can tell me a little more about the lovely Highlands, and dams and things. As it's so early. Come along, Clarissa.'

The lady-in-waiting, a thin rather exhausted-looking girl, correctly described by Rory as 'high-born but downtrodden like all Sophie's slaves,' leapt to her feet. It was a royal command. And for that matter, a royal victory.

'Henry, you really shouldn't have—' began Lady Edith, immediately the much-enlarged royal party had left.

'Brilliant, Dad,' said Kim Beauregard.

'Shut up, Edith,' replied Colonel Henry in a perfectly equable voice. 'Kim—bed!'

Jemima wondered who on earth was going to take her home. She gathered Father Flanagan was staying the night in order to say Mass in the morning at Kilbronnack. She watched Colonel Henry at the drinks tray. She distinctly saw him put a bottle of whisky in his pocket before he turned around.

'And now, Miss Shore, I shall escort you back to the Wild Island,' he said. Lady Edith's mouth opened and then shut. For an instant Father Flanagan was seen to frown. But nobody, including Jemima Shore, had the courage to contradict the Colonel.

Jemima thought of the *Express* headline quoted by the

Princess? IS SHE SAFE? At that moment it seemed more appropriate to her own fate, returning alone to a deserted place with a man she strongly suspected of being a murderer, than to that of the pampered Princess, surrounded by her youthful admirers in the Railway Hotel.

TWELVE

Midnight and After

Colonel Henry relaxed with a whisky in his hand. It was his third since their arrival at Eilean Fas.

Jemima stretched out one leg toward the fire. The green jersey of her skirt fell away, revealing her dark sheer stockings and green slippers—neither of them particularly suitable for Scotland. With the tip of her slipper she had just drawn a heart in the dust now thickly forming in the grate. A dirty mark resulted on the toe of her slipper: in London her precise soul would have felt sullied by the imperfection; here she felt strangely uncaring.

Several plans had been made, all delightful, for Highland diversions, from fishing (Jemima was not too keen, with her memories of Charles Beauregard and his waders), to grouse-shooting. But what about the poor grouse—

'Oh, there aren't any worth mentioning to feel sorry for up here,' said the Colonel airily. 'We only talk about them in the first place in order to let the shooting for a decent rent. To be frank,' he added, 'it's the tenants you should feel sorry for. At our rates.'

Finally, on discovering that it was her birthday at the end of the week, the Colonel settled on some form of expedition then. 'August 30th. Virgo,' said Jemima lightly. She did not imagine the Colonel paid much attention to the stars. Nor indeed did she, except to enjoy from time to time the double image of her own sign, the cool white maiden on the one hand, the harvest goddess reigning over the most fertile time of the year on the other. Sometimes she was aware of these two images, the desire for self-preservation and for self-abandon, combining, even fighting in herself.

She was wrong about the Colonel.

'I'm a Scorpio,' he informed her. 'Very sexy.' It was said as a statement of fact. He added: 'August 30th. I think old Edith's birthday is somewhere around there. Might even *be* August 30th. Anyway, we'll do something.'

'And if it is Edith's birthday?'

'Edith and the boys. Oh, they might have their own picnic,' he replied vaguely. 'With Father Flanagan. That's what Edith and the boys would like.

'You know, Jemima,' he said, in his curious individual clipped diction, 'I loved my brother Carlo more than anyone on this earth. And since he died, nothing has ever been quite the same again. I believe I loved him even more than this glen—because to me he *was* the Glen.'

On hearing this surprising—because it was so deeply affectionate—remark about his brother, Jemima withdrew her leg, lazily. 'I thought you hated each other,' she said. The whisky the Colonel had persuaded her to share was taking effect.

'Ah.' The Colonel paused and looked reflectively into the fire. His own even longer legs were also stretched out in the direction of the smouldering logs. They were both seated, at a suitable distance, on the same sofa. 'Ah,' he repeated, 'I detect the hand of Clementina.' Then: 'She's unbalanced, of course, my niece. Deranged. Mad. Whatever you like to call it. Like her mother before her. Like her lunatic drug-taking brother.'

He poured another whisky. 'All that rot about hating Carlo and hating Charles, and finally murdering him. What absolute nonsense! Don't tell me she actually took you in, woman of the world.

'My God, I've given my whole life to looking after this place for Charles, haven't I? Could have got a good job in the City, chap I knew in the war offered me one, more money, better for poor Edith in every way. But no, I thought it was my duty to stay up here and look after the Estate. What Carlo would have wanted...

'I tell you, it was the happiest day of my life when Leonie told me she was pregnant. Made the terrible blow of Carlo's death bearable, d'you know, to think there would be something of his to carry on. I was always sure it would be a boy, quite convinced of it. All that time, nearly eight months we waited, I was sure I was holding the Estate in trust for little Charles, my brother's son. No idea Leonie was having twins, of course. My family have never had twins.' There was even a shade of indignation in the last remark.

'Wasn't Clementina actually born first?'

'She was. Oh God, I said, when the doctor told us. And Edith fell on her knees and prayed.' He paused again, sipping his drink, lost in the contemplation of that strange scene thirty years ago.

'Getting back to my unfortunate niece and her ravings, I really don't know what to do about it. Getting to my wits' end with her, especially now she's got the Red Rose behind her, letting them use Castle Beauregard as their headquarters. Lachlan's not a bad lad at heart, he was corrupted by my nephew, father a very decent type, served with me in the war, but some of the people with Lachlan I don't like the look of.

'I wanted to ask your advice about it all, as a matter of fact. Do you think she should see a doctor of sorts? An analyst perhaps? That kind of thing. Did think of a doctor for Charles, but that was different. But maybe a psychiatrist would straighten out Clementina and remove this obsession about her father, and me, and her brother's death and the whole damn shooting match. There was a fellow I knew in the war, wonderful when the troops cracked up under fire. I don't know if he's still around.'

It was well after midnight. Otherwise this complete reinterpretation of family events in Glen Bronnack might have come as even more of a shock to Jemima Shore.

As it was, she allowed herself to be poured yet another whisky. She suspected it was going—had already gone—to her head. Whose version was to be believed? It all reminded her of *Rashomon*, a film she was apt to recall in any case from time to time when carrying out one of her television investigations.

On the one hand Colonel Henry painted a most plausible if painful picture of a young heir growing to manhood under his uncle's loving tutelage. On the other hand he delineated a character, from the start gravely flawed, and furthermore spoiled to death by his unbalanced American mother.

'She must have had bad blood in her, poor Leonie, and passed it on to the twins. God knows she was unstable enough,' exclaimed the Colonel bitterly. 'As for Charles, no Beauregard was ever like that before. I tried to understand, tried to be tolerant. Even Edith thought I was too soft with him. I certainly treated him much softer than my own kids. Fatherless boy and all that, my own brother's son. Always difficult to be the son of a hero into the bargain. But the rot started early. He was vicious, my nephew Charles, no other word for it. Either he couldn't stick the school or the school couldn't keep him. In the end I prevailed on poor Father Flanagan to give him a few lessons up here, up at the Castle; at least he could put the fear of God into him from his enormous height. Charles was not much taller than Clementina, whereas the men of my family have always been over six foot tall.

'Later of course it was hopeless. Drugs, that sort of thing. Don't really want to go into it now, *de mortuis*, don't you know. In spite of that, in spite of the Castle becoming a kind of cesspool, a refuge for every addict and long-haired pansy with nowhere else to go, in spite of the Red Rose, why, he even uprooted the famous Beauregard white rose garden, the white circle, and planted some fearful crimson number, some appalling floribunda of the most dreadfully vulgar colour! Edith nearly had a fit. Wonderful gardener, old Edith. Loves flowers. Leonie never had a clue about what you could and couldn't do in that respect. Have you noticed how American gardens are never quite right? Where was I?'

The Colonel was visibly bristling. In a calmer voice he went on, 'Yes, in spite of the Red Rose (and all his foul red roses) I still didn't want him dead. He was my own brother's son,' Colonel Henry concluded for the third time.

That was the Colonel's version of events. On the other hand there was Clementina's directly opposing story of a wicked uncle waiting his chance to scoop his nephew's inheritance. How on earth was she to decide?

'The film, *Brother Raiders*!' exclaimed Jemima.

'Oh, did you see it?' A pleased smile crossed the Colonel's handsome face. He arched his neck and shot the frill of his shirt still further out of his sleeve. 'I was pretty good, wasn't I?'

'Kirk Douglas—' began Jemima hesitantly.

'Gregory Peck!' replied the Colonel indignantly. 'Kirk Douglas looks nothing like me.'

'Sorry,' she said with haste. 'Yes, you were very good indeed. What I wondered was—you must have made some money out of it all, at least I hope you did, it was a colossally successful film, what happened to it?'

'Of course I made money out of it. Not a complete fool. That was the money that paid for the Beauregard Memorial Hall at Kilbronnack. Somewhere for the people round here to meet on Saturday night; show films, dance. What Carlo would have wanted. So much better than Charlie's idiotic notion of a museum on an island, incidentally: who needs that? Leonie was going to build it originally, but after we—er—fell out—'

He paused, evidently at a slight loss how to phrase his next remarks. 'Such a pretty woman,' he went on. 'When she was young, a little fairy. Clementina looks just like her. And talks just like her. But mad. So intense about everything she did. No lightness. She seriously thought I would leave Edith for her; well, how could I? Four boys already, another on the way, my sister-in-law, the Catholic Church, and all that. It was never on.

'Of course I was an idiot too, come to think of it,' added the Colonel reflectively. 'I should never have got involved. Father Flanagan really pitched into me about it all. He was a young priest then, but with a tongue like a whip-lash which he didn't hesitate to use. The trouble is I've never been able to resist—' he coughed. 'Well, anyway, after that she hated me. Used to shout things at me if I met her in Kilbronnack. Then it calmed down. And then—well, she died.'

That too sounded very plausible. Jemima Shore was beginning to suspect that wilfully or otherwise Clementina Beauregard had conned her into believing a totally false version of events. No doubt Clementina herself had been conned in the first place by her own mother, and later by her brother. It still did not add up to a very pretty story. Even the girl's dog was half mad if not vicious. If Flora really had sprung at Bridie on the bridge, could Clementina even have encouraged her to do so?

The fire, which they had relit on their return, was beginning to die down. Colonel Henry bent down and threw on another log. Sparks flew up, and his silver buttons flashed in the sudden bright light. He sat back and looked directly at Jemima. For an instant it was an extremely level look, half sardonic, half tender. Then he smiled:

'Finish family,' he said. 'Now tell me about you.' Leaning forward, he took Jemima's glass from her fingers.

'You've had enough, I think.' So saying, he poured himself another large dram of whisky.

A detail struck Jemima.

'The note!' she cried. 'Your note to Ben, telling him that Charles would be at Marjorie's Pool the afternoon he died; you said he was beginning to suspect something.'

The Colonel looked startled, but not particularly perturbed. 'Oh, that. How did you hear about it?' he said. 'Well, that little plot was overtaken by events all right. Ben was going to tackle Charles about seeing a doctor to help him get off drugs. And Ossian Lucas had arranged to bring this doctor, this friend of his, up to the Highlands, as though on holiday. The point was, we didn't want Charles to think there was a conspiracy to help him, particularly not with me involved. The choice had to come from him, the doctor said.'

Once again, the Colonel sounded plausible enough.

'Now I really insist on talking about you,' he said. 'You're a very beautiful woman. Hair like sunshine. And eyes like a cat: what an extraordinary colour they are. But you've been told that before many times, I've no doubt.'

He touched her cheek, and then her hair lightly. Jemima noticed once again that he had the most surprisingly long fingers and elegant hands for such a masculine-looking man. For a moment she thought he would touch her further. She felt herself tremble.

'Never before in the Highlands of Scotland,' she replied in the lightest tone she could muster. Jemima was still trying to decide what she would do if the Colonel tried to kiss her—scream? struggle? remain coolly passive?—when he moved suddenly and pressed his lips down very hard on hers, thus making further decisions on the subject unnecessary. In the event, she neither screamed nor struggled, nor, she discovered, did she remain coolly passive.

'I've been longing to do that for the last half hour,' said the Colonel, when they were finally apart, and gazing at each other, each panting slightly. 'I've been drinking all this whisky, and talking about the past, and all the time I've been trying to muster up courage to make a pass at you. I must have drunk at least five whiskies.'

'Mightn't *too* much whisky be a slight mistake? Under the circumstances,' queried Jemima, her boldness surprising herself.

'Certainly not. Whisky is mother's milk for us Scots,' replied the Colonel. Then he placed his hand on her left breast, the nipple prominent under the thin wool, and bent his lips towards it. With his other hand he began to caress her thigh, from the point of the suspender upwards.

Much later Jemima said, 'You were right about the whisky. It didn't make any difference at all.'

'How can you tell?' answered Henry Beauregard sleepily. 'You don't know what I'm like without it.'

'When shall I know that?' enquired Jemima in an equally lazy voice. The fire had died down. The lights were out. The room she knew must be strewn with such diverse objects as buckled shoes (his), green slippers (hers), dark stockings (hers), tartan socks (his), a variety of white underwear, some satin and lacy, some plain and poplin. To say nothing of larger objects like a black kilt jacket and a green jersey dress. The kilt itself had been thrown lightly over both of them by its owner, when he felt for a cigarette, 'Nothing like a kilt for warmth.' It *was* warm. Altogether Jemima felt very warm indeed and secure.

'In the morning of course. No whisky around at that time of day. Come along. I'm going to take you and myself upstairs to that enormous and, as I remember it, very comfortable bed. You'll find out what I'm like in the morning.'

But Jemima Shore never did find out. In the morning, when she awoke, she was alone in the enormous bed. It was Ben Beauregard, not the Colonel, who was bending over her, touching her shoulder.

'Miss Shore,' he was saying. 'I'm terribly sorry to disturb you like this. But where's Dad? He's completely disappeared.'

THIRTEEN

'I'll Be Back'

Because it was—for her—early in the morning and because Jemima was not immediately awake, her first thought
was a purely feminine pang of regret. Sleepily, confused,
she thought: he has gone, but he promised to stay.
Morning had come and her night lover had fled as Cupid
had fled from Psyche to avoid the dangerous contact of the
dawn, and yet he had promised . . .

Then Ben Beauregard was saying something of more
immediate import: 'We think the Red Rose has got him.
We found a bunch of red roses on the doorstep of
Kilbronnack House this morning. Plus their ridiculous
sign: UR2. Ugh, reminds me of some kind of nuclear
weapon. And their slogans: Long Live Queen Clementina
the First! Down with the Usurper Henry Beauregard!
Eilean Fas the Royal Island.'

Her mind began to clear. The Red Rose had struck
indeed: not after all at a Princess guarded at Inverness by

her police and detectives and minions, but at the hated local laird, the man they regarded as the purloiner of his niece's rights, the murderer of his royal nephew . . . It all made a kind of hideous sense.

Then her mind cleared still further. He had gone. A new aspect of it all struck her. Where he had gone was one question due to be investigated, but, to be blunt, *when* he had gone was now her paramount concern. She gazed at Ben, at his handsome face with its thick crest of dark hair. She did not, for the moment, have the courage to look at the bed beside her.

'He brought me home last night—' she began rather uncertainly.

'Oh, we know that,' Ben appeared to dismiss that episode with carelessness. 'Mum told us that. But you see, it's so unlike Dad not to be home for breakfast. Even if it's a very late breakfast.' He spoke rapidly, almost impatiently, as if this simple fact must be well known to everybody. The picture conjured up by this generalization was more than Jemima felt able to contemplate for the time being.

'Then there came the call—' he went on. 'Anonymous. Didn't recognize the voice. But the message was clear enough—"If you want to get back the usurper Henry Beauregard, you had better come over to Castle Beauregard straight away."'

Jemima decided that there were two, no three, things that she needed immediately to fortify her before she faced further shocks to her system. What was it indeed about the north of Scotland that she was constantly being aroused by dramatic events brought literally into her very bedroom? Poor Bridie, Lachlan, Clementina, now Ben, there was scarcely a minute's peace in her Paradise. The first two things were orange juice and coffee. The third was a dressing-gown. Jemima was suddenly aware that beneath the thick hairy blankets of the old-fashioned bed she was wearing nothing at all. At least Clementina had found her in a satin nightdress. She decided to shoo Ben Beauregard downstairs.

'Look, I'll meet you in the drawing room and tell you all I know. But do you think—possibly—some coffee? And there's some juice in the larder...' Smoothing her remarkably tousled hair back, Jemima smiled beguilingly at Ben. But where Guthrie Carlyle would have leapt at her command—no, to be frank, Guthrie would have already brought the juice, he never even called her without a glass of chilled orange juice in his hand—Ben Beauregard simply stood there gazing at her.

'Coffee?' he said blankly. She might have been asking him to grow the stuff. It occurred to Jemima that this fashion-plate of Highland masculine beauty had probably never in his life been asked to perform such a mundane task. She spared a cross thought for the cosseting Lady Edith, whose gift to the modern world was apparently six totally undomesticated sons. As well as being herself a highly understanding wife... Although it was a pity that Carrie Amyas, wife of Tom, had never had the accommodating nature of Lady Edith Beauregard. Jemima—the memory of those inevitable if late breakfasts still rankling—wondered for the first time whether it was not possible for wives to be too understanding. Ignoring that line of thought as unprofitable before coffee, she decided it was not part of her business to teach Ben Beauregard what his mother had signally failed to do. Particularly at such a critical juncture.

'Wait downstairs then.'

He went.

It was while Jemima was in the process of tying her dark blue silk kimono tightly round her that she found the note. It was written on a scrap of paper which looked like a fly-leaf torn hastily from an old book. She recognized the handwriting from the note which Clementina had shown her. It said quite simply: 'I'll be back. H.B.B.'

And that was all. Which got her precisely nowhere, except to inform her that the Colonel's departure had evidently—if unflatteringly—been voluntary. It was not even all that unflattering if you took into account his avowed intention, not yet carried out, to return. As for his departure being voluntary, that was not exactly a surprise: deep sleeper as she might be, particularly under certain agreeable circumstances, including the unaccustomed draughts of whisky, she could never have believed that Colonel Henry had been abducted literally from her side without waking her.

So why had he gone voluntarily into the power of the Red Rose? And who had summoned him? And how?

Later in the drawing room, over coffee for two made by Jemima and drunk happily but not particularly gratefully by Ben, she said, 'And since then, no word?'

'You were our last hope. Mum said I should check first.' Ben's tone changed. 'He wasn't—of course it sounds silly—I suppose he wasn't taken forcibly from here, was he?' For a moment Jemima did not understand why he sounded embarrassed. She looked down. He was holding one of the Colonel's silver gilt buttons in his hand; he was not exactly extending it towards her, more twisting it in his hand. He had, presumably, found it on the hearthrug or thereabouts.

'No, nothing forcible took place here,' replied Jemima in her most even voice. There eyes met. Behind Jemima's ironic regard lurked the ghost of a smile. Ben Beauregard returned it.

'Then I'd better tackle my fair cousin Clementina in her castle lair. No, correction, in our castle lair.'

Jemima took a decision.

'No, we'll both do that. I have one or two questions to ask Queen Clementina myself.'

She did not at this point care to mention the commission given to her by Clementina Beauregard, and, it had to be said, tacitly accepted by Jemima Shore: a commission of investigation into the murder of Charles Beauregard in which Henry Beauregard was the prime suspect. Now not only was Henry Beauregard vindicated by his transformation into the victim but, as regards the second local death—the apparently accidental death of Bridie Stuart—Jemima was beginning to have hideous doubts as to whether Clementina herself might not be implicated. The presence of the dog Flora could not be easily dismissed. The girl was surely crazy enough for anything, with her accusations, her obsessions, and now her involvement with the more way-out form of Scottish Nationalism, including a possible kidnapping.

Charles Beauregard had taken drugs; during Jemima's one and only encounter with Clementina, the girl had depended on nothing more lethal than a vast quantity of Rothman's cigarettes in a very short time. That proved nothing. The habit of drug-taking was easily inculcated.

In jeans, brown cowboy boots and a thin cream-coloured jersey under her white Burberry, Jemima hoped she would present a formidable aspect to Queen Clementina.

It was, however, Castle Beauregard which presented the formidable aspect. Seen from the shores of the loch, as they drove up the winding path to its eminence, it began to remind her of the castle in the Disney film *Snow White*, the first film she had ever seen and thus she supposed inevitably one of the formative visual influences in her life.

Whoever built it had not spared a Victorian/mediaeval detail. Quite apart from the flowering and springing buttresses and turrets, there was even a drawbridge and a portcullis.

From the battlements hung a flag together with various other trophy-like objects of indeterminate nature.

'Imagine building this!' exclaimed Jemima. 'One wonders what the original castle looked like.'

'The site of the old Castle Tamh was slightly different. To the north: like all old Scottish dwellings, seeking shelter from the wind, as well as the enemy. Where the garden now is. The old castle itself was knocked down in the sixteenth century. The Frasers or some local despots came and blitzed it during one of their endless feuds. A heap of masonry was all that remained on the site. Bonnie Prince Charlie and Sighing Marjorie are supposed to have trysted in the ruins—before Culloden, when her father was still alive and too busy chaperoning her for any hanky-panky to take place at Eilean Fas. By now all the stones have been used for garden seats and grottoes and sun-dials, etc etc, in the white rose garden.'

He paused and said very angrily, stepping on the accelerator of the Land-Rover, '*Red* rose garden. But it won't be for much longer. We'll change all that. The white roses will be back at Castle Beauregard next summer. Even if it costs a packet to replace them. You'll see.' As Colonel Henry had said, he would be back. The Beauregards had a taste for return.

'Tell me about the Beauregard Armoury. Young Duncan mentioned it,' Jemima said to change the subject.

'Collected by my great-grandfather,' replied Ben. 'Worth a fortune.' Jemima noticed with curiosity that the value of absolutely anything was never far from Ben's conversation: the relic no doubt of his poverty-stricken over-brothered childhood. Or was it a Scottish characteristic? But she had never heard Guthrie Carlyle make a single reference to the monetary value of anything—only to the artistic value of anything and, late at night after a good deal of red wine, to the moral value of everything.

'God knows what Clementina and her gang of local layabouts led by Lachlan have done with the guns,' he concluded. 'Sold them no doubt.'

As if in direct and contradictory answer to Ben's off-hand remark, there was a sharp crack, and then another, a sound more like an explosion than a bullet. At what seemed to be one and the same moment, the Land-Rover slewed violently to the left and into the ditch beside the narrow road leading up to the Castle. Jemima was jolted violently and ended up falling across Ben Beauregard.

There was the sound of running feet and a group of men appeared, surrounding the Land-Rover. Among them Lachlan was prominent. He went to the driving seat. Another man, whom Jemima vaguely recognized, opened the door of the Land-Rover from the left and made a grab towards her. He had red hair and a thin face, paler than the rest of his associates—or perhaps it was the hair which empha-sized his pallor.

The familiar rose-and-bloodstained T-shirts were back in force. But it was symptomatic of the new violence of the occasion that there were no flowers now behind their ears. There was one much older man present, inappropriately dressed in a T-shirt. Jemima suddenly recognized Young Duncan.

At the wheel Ben Beauregard was struggling violently, and so frenetic were his gestures that Jemima was terrified the already listing Land-Rover would heel over completely. Above their heads the portcullis gate yawned; could those heavy iron spikes which fringed it actually be for real? There was another flag, a placard with something written on it in Gaelic, and a dangling heavy object supporting another placard.

'Aye, Lachlan, tie him up and take them both into the Castle,' said the red-haired man in a tone of authority. 'Then we'll pull up the drawbridge.' Jemima suddenly remembered him as the somewhat mysterious figure who had entered and left St. Margaret's by the side door on the day of the funeral.

'Leave us alone,' cried Jemima, desperately beginning to struggle in her turn as she saw some hefty ropes being applied—not gently at all—to Ben Beauregard. One of the ropes, intentionally or not, was drawn across his mouth and acted as a kind of gag. 'Leave him alone. You're tearing him. Oh God. Wherever is Colonel Henry?' she added in a voice more like a wail than a cry. 'Colonel Henry would soon sort you all out.'

'Aye, you may well ask that, Miss Jemima Shore,' commented Lachlan, 'seeing as you have now joined the ranks of his numerous wummin and strumpets.' There was a note of vicious prurience, a horrid gloating delight in his voice. He came around the Land-Rover to her side and, taking her two hands, jerked them quite savagely behind her. His eyes, small, cold and blue, gazed at her in a way which was both disapproving and covetous. The respect he had shown to her on all previous occasions had quite gone. He addressed her, Jemima thought suddenly, in a confused mixed image, as John Knox might have addressed the woman taken in adultery. Half disapprovingly. Half lustfully.

'How dare you touch her?' Ben's voice under the rope was glottal, strangled, but still violent.

'If we were mindful to touch her, which we are not, there's no a thing you can do about it, Mr. Ben Beauregard,' said the red-haired man in a voice full of contempt. 'It's the Red Rose is in power here, not the laird, I'll have ye know.'

'In the absence of Colonel Henry, where is Miss Beauregard herself?' enquired Jemima in the coolest voice she could muster. 'I demand to be taken before her.'

The men exchanged looks. Lachlan whispered with the

red-haired man. There appeared to be some form of divided command.

'Aeneas and I agree that we'll take you to her,' said Lachlan.

'And what's going to happen to Mr. Ben?' pursued Jemima.

Lachlan, the man called Aeneas and the rest, even Young Duncan, favoured Ben with a sardonic quizzical stare. There was a short laugh from someone.

'Him. Aye, mebbe we'll send him to join his father,' said one of them.

'And where might that be?' The pretence of boldness had made Jemima actually feel bolder. By way of reply, Lachlan jerked his thumb upwards.

With a feeling of total nausea, Jemima realized that the heavy object revolving slowly in the wind above them, hanging upright from the battlements, was in fact a body: a body wearing a jacket of black velvet on which no doubt there were silver buttons, a body wearing a kilt. Colonel Henry Beauregard would not after all be able to keep his promise to her to return.

FOURTEEN

Danger

Rope serrating the corners of his mouth, Ben Beauregard continued to stare upwards at the body of his father swinging above their heads from the portcullis. To Jemima, he seemed extraordinarily cool.

'It's the dummy,' he said, his voice strangled but still audible. 'The dummy from the castle attic. Uncle Carlo and Dad had it made for target practice when they were boys. She dressed it up. A shabby trick.'

Jemima found she was trembling violently. Tears had begun to form in her eyes. She wanted to control them.

'It's maybe a dummy, a grand stuffed body, but it's a warning to you all the same,' commented the man called Aeneas grimly. 'So shall all the lairds hang one day from the battlements when the Red Rose reigns over Scotland. And the Scottish people shall enjoy the freedom of their own land: with no lairds to harry them and drive them from their crofts.' It sounded like the beginning of a speech.

'A new Scotland under the rule of their new sovereign her Majesty Queen Clementina,' added Lachlan quickly, rather too quickly, interrupting him.

'Up the Red Rose,' chimed in Duncan, 'and may the White run Red. Colonel Henry was ever a reasonable man. I'm sure he'll be joining the Red Rose any day now and giving us our lodges for our own. There's no one I'd sooner work for than the Colonel, if I owned my own wee lodge.'

Relief was gradually calming the trembling of Jemima's limbs. Her mind too was regaining its alertness. It was clear to her that even within the gun-laden party now marching towards the vast baronial door of the Castle there were three shades of opinion. While Aeneas, surname and origins unknown, concentrated on the land-for-the-people aspect of Scottish independence—in Jacobin as well as Jacobite terms—Lachlan had from their first meeting shown a kind of romanticism, even reverence, of a very different order. As for Young Duncan, Jemima remembered his fervent recitation of the slogan of the Red Rose on her original journey up the valley. What she had then taken for sycophancy was evidently conviction—of a sort. But Young Duncan's conviction was strictly from the point of view of his own prosperity. He had no further axe to grind, no animus against his employer Colonel Henry and no particular reverence for Queen Clementina.

The man called Aeneas equated the Red Rose with the Red Flag—social revolution, in short. For Lachlan Stuart, son of the dead Bridie with her Beauregard loyalties, the two flags were worlds apart.

So must the earlier army of Prince Charles Edward Stuart also have been divided, into revolutionaries, romantics and self-seekers...

The sight of the enormous entrance hall to Castle Beauregard obliterated these thoughts for the time being. Here was the Beauregard Armoury in all its martial splendour. Circles, whorls and cascading spirals of guns and other weapons were pinioned to the walls. Guns were not the sole weapons displayed. Gleaming knives, long pikes, vicious-looking bayonets demonstrated the long history of the art of war. The few weapons of defence exhibited—a shield or two from an earlier age—looked oddly out of place. The martial spirit as interpreted by the Beauregard Armoury was pre-eminently one of attack, not defence.

Here and there the elaborate artistry with which the armoury had been arranged on the walls had been despoiled. A number of guns were missing from their positions as the spokes of a series of rising wheels directly abutting the general's picture. These were the guns in the hands of Lachlan, Aeneas and their companions which continued to menace Ben and Jemima as they trod warily through the hall.

The impression of mediaeval vastness did not fade as the party left the hall and began to ascend a broad stone staircase, on the walls of which huge flags of indeterminate royal and Scottish nature were hung. No expense of royal Victorian spirit had been spared in building this fantasy palace.

Lachlan stuck a thumb in the direction of a narrow arch giving a glimpse of descending stone steps.

'That way to the dungeon,' he said. After a moment Jemima realized that he was not joking. As they reached the crest of the great staircase, two portraits dominated the entrance to what was presumably the Great Drawing Room. Or the Great Library. It scarcely needed the gold label affixed to the ornate frame to inform Jemima that here was the founding father of the Beauregard family—if you believed the legend—Bonnie Prince Charlie himself.

Only, this portrait was in itself a Victorian fantasy. Magnificent in tartan, many different shades and patterns of it combined, bedizened with sporran, plaid, dirks and daggers, Celtic brooches and the rest, as well as Victorian whiskers, moustache and beard, his Majesty King Charles III (as the label termed him) was depicted as a portly nine-teenth-century Stuart. The background of the picture contained a large red velvet throne and a couple of dogs, too lean for labradors, straining at leashes held by a couple of tartan-clad retainers. No, thought Jemima, life up the Glen for Bonnie Prince Charlie was never like this; but the picture would do very nicely on a whisky bottle.

There was a companion piece, equally splendidly Victorian in its concept and execution. Here Sighing Marjorie—for it could be no other—with flowing chestnut hair, a baby in her arms, delicate white gown and tartan shawl, cowered over a waterfall while a force of red-coated soldiers stood rather woodenly by. The background of this picture consisted of a vivid impression of Castle Beauregard at sunset. Looking at the leading soldier's stolid expression, Jemima was irresistibly tempted to caption it: 'Go on, jump then.'

Entering the Great Library, her first surprise was to rediscover immediately the red velvet throne featured in the Prince's picture.

Clementina Beauregard was seated negligently on it, her pale face and hair set off by the crimson canopy louring over her head. She was smoking the stub of a cigarette. The curtains, heavy, somnolent-seeming plum-coloured curtains, were still drawn. The room was full of smoke and had a recognizable semi-sweet reek. As the heavy oak door to the library swung open, the sound of a Rolling Stones record, not in its first youth and played very loud, blared in their faces.

In all this noise and smoky darkness, for a moment the fairy-like delicacy of Clementina provided a strange contrast. Yet there was a hint of fancy dress in her own costume. On second thoughts, she did not look so out of place in the Great Library after all. In spite of the hour, Clementina was wearing a long red dress of panne velvet, too big for her and slightly Edwardian in cut, with a type of bustle and tight leg o'mutton sleeves from which most of the buttons were missing. She also wore a black hat, even more dilapidated, but with traces of grandiose feathers and flowers on its brim. Ropes of pale pink pearls hung down across her tiny bosom, which swelled out the red velvet hardly perceptibly. Some of the pearls were peeling or had lost their pinkness altogether.

Above her loomed another vast portrait, this time of an imposing female rather than a male. Built on a far ampler scale, this former Beauregard beauty was wearing identical costume to that of her descendant Clementina, seated beneath her imperious gaze. Did this adoption of the semi-regal outfit of her ancestress indicate that Clementina had decided to put on some sort of show to receive her captives?

If so, the impulse had passed. Clementina's eyes were fixed unwaveringly on Ben. She did not seem to take in the presence of Jemima. Swiftly, she knocked rather than switched the record player into silence. It was lying on the corner of the dais to the throne; there was a morass of records, none of them looking particularly well cared for, within reach.

'So, Ben, come to take over, have you?' she said in a voice which was considerably slowed down from her usual frenetic diction. 'Castle first, then the island, and last of all pretty cousin Clementina.' Her voice trailed away. She took a brief drag on the cigarette stub in her fingers. From the smell of the room, clinging round the dark curtains and recesses of the library, not strongly but unmistakably,

Jemima guessed that she had been smoking the marijuana for hours, maybe all night.

Lamps with dark green pleated shades illuminated the library and there were other pictures to be seen among the books. The exquisite fair-haired lady over the fireplace, a romantic post-war portrait with the Castle in the background—John Merton perhaps?—was so strikingly like Clementina as to be readily identifiable as Leonie Beauregard. There were photographs as well. One pair of portraits, carefully juxtaposed, demonstrated the rakes' progress of the Beauregard twins. On the one hand a carefully posed picture, unmistakably by Cecil Beaton, showed them as soulful and curly-haired angels at their mother's knee: Charles in frilly shirt and satin page's trousers, Clementina in high-waisted flounced dress and sash. The second portrait, by David Bailey, showed a couple of unadorned faces, placed close together, the expressions both pagan and mocking.

Everything in Castle Beauregard, however ancestral, was also highly painted, decorated and where appropriate varnished. The pictures looked as if they had been newly cleaned. The plum-coloured curtains, with their magnificent dark swags of material and tasselled gold fringes, did not look old. The carpets were thick and soft, as well as being tartan, a combination which put the thought into Jemima's mind that Leonie Beauregard's American money must be responsible for the splendour. For one thing, the interior of the Castle, stone-built as it might be, was not particularly cold. The library was positively hot, yet the log fire was not lit. Was it possible to centrally heat a castle, and in August? There was a strange southern warmth about the place.

Not only the warmth but also the good, even brilliant, state of repair of the Castle itself contrasted markedly with the shabbiness of that other Beauregard residence at Kilbronnack, to say nothing of the ruined state of Eilean

Fas. Every visit to the Castle by the junior branch of the Beauregards must have rubbed in the contrast epitomized by Dives and Lazarus—Dives: Charles, the heir; Lazarus: Ben and all his siblings.

'Have a smoke,' said Clementina suddenly, extending the stub to Jemima, who shook her head. At which Clementina half minced, half staggered towards Ben and stuck the stub between his lips. Ben did not move. Jemima admired his control once more: the only uncontrolled thing about him she could detect was a vein beating on the side of his temple. After a moment Clementina removed the stub and, standing on tip-toe, put her velvet-clad arms round her cousin's neck. Then she kissed him lightly, on the lips. Ben still did not move.

'Pretty pretty cousin Clementina,' she repeated. 'Don't you want to kiss her now, Ben? So pretty.' Once again her words sounded slurred.

She turned to Jemima.

'He wanted to kiss me once. He wanted to very much. I didn't tell you that, did I?'

'There are quite a lot of things you didn't tell me,' answered Jemima grimly. 'In fact I'm beginning to think you told me a pack of lies the other day at breakfast. Though why you should take the trouble—'

Clementina giggled, tottered back to the huge sofa by the fireplace—Jemima noticed she was wearing black satin buckled shoes, much too big for her—and threw herself backwards onto it.

'Then I'll tell you the truth now,' she said, still laughing. 'We've plenty of time. While they're getting Uncle Henry to sign the paper giving Eilean Fas for a Memorial Island. And cousin Ben here to back him up. We need that island, the Red Rose needs it. Good for morals. I mean morale. That's what he says. Good for morale.' There were more giggles.

'I'll be glad to hear the truth,' replied Jemima carefully. 'But why don't you get Lachlan to release Ben while you're talking? These ropes surely aren't necessary inside the Castle.'

'But I adore the ropes!' cried Clementina with enthusiasm. 'So kinky. Don't you adore ropes, cousin Ben, darling?' Then there was another change of mood and she said quite sharply: 'Lachlan, untie Mr. Ben at once. Untie him, I said. And then go and get us some champagne from the cellar. The crystal champagne. We must have some champagne to celebrate. And fetch Uncle Henry too—if he's being good that is—he can celebrate too.'

Celebrate what? Jemima wondered.

'I've got no orders to fetch the Colonel from the dungeons,' said Lachlan in what for him was a surly voice. He looked at Aeneas, who shook his head.

'Orders, whose orders are you talking about?' replied Clementina petulantly. 'It's my orders now at the Castle.' She tapped her small foot in its bent black shoe, so that the paste buckle rattled. Then it fell off. Clementina paid no attention.

'Our Chief's orders, your Majesty.' Lachlan gazed quite steadily at Clementina as he spoke.

They were interrupted by the shrill sound of the telephone, a sound to which Jemima found that she had grown so unaccustomed that the ordinary urban noise made her start as though at a tocsin. Clementina seemed uncertain what to do. Then she staggered over to the instrument and picked up the receiver. She said nothing. Someone was speaking rapidly at the other end. Jemima could hear the voice, but not the words.

'Is it the Chief now?' asked Aeneas intensely.

Clementina gave one of her high laughs, nodded, said into the telephone, 'Then you'd better give the warning straight away.' She listened briefly and dropped the receiver without saying goodbye.

'Fancy that,' she added to the assembled company. 'Fancy that. The Chief is a very worried man. He's coming over here himself. Says he's got something very important to tell me. Danger. He's talking about danger. I may be in danger. What does he mean? How can I be in danger? I'm with the Red Rose, aren't I? I'm their Queen. Cousin Ben's in danger and Uncle Henry's in danger. Even Miss Jemima Shore is in a little bit of danger if the Red Rose turns nasty—naughty Miss Shore carrying on with wicked Uncle Henry. But how can Queen Clementina the First be in danger? Oh, Lachlan, do get the crystal champagne, I want to celebrate. I want to celebrate my accession.'

Ah, thought Jemima, so that's what we're celebrating.

'He mustn't be seen,' said Lachlan in a hard voice. 'He won't want the prisoners catching sight of him. You know his orders. That would be dangerous.'

'Danger! Danger! Give me your answer do. Who's afraid of the big bad danger, the big bad danger,' Clementina sang in a high, rather pretty voice. 'I think I'll put on another record.'

She put on the record of 'Satisfaction.'

'I can't get any danger out of you,' Clementina sang above the notes of the record.

Jemima thought they were all in danger, from Colonel Henry in his dungeon to herself in the power of a nest of lunatics. Even Clementina, the alternative Queen of Scotland, had apparently something to fear. She also wondered who the Chief might be—and whether his existence increased or diminished the danger.

FIFTEEN

Official Action

'Where was the Chief telephoning from?' asked Lachlan aggressively.

'There were pips,' said Clementina rather vaguely. 'Pip, pip, pip. So it can't have been,' she stopped, 'you know where.'

With a jerk of his head, Aeneas left the room taking Ben with him, the gun held to his back. Ben offered no resistance. It was difficult to see how he could have done so: he had presumably gone to join his father in the dungeons. That left Lachlan—and his gun—against Jemima. Clementina, who had wandered back to her throne, plucking some of the flowers from her hat as she did so and casting them aside in an Ophelia-like gesture, remained an uncertain quantity.

'So you'll be staying quiet, Miss Shore,' said Lachlan after Ben had gone, reverting to his vicious tone. 'Till we decide what to do with you. That'll be understood, will it not? Otherwise it's your paramour, the Colonel, who will suffer.'

Jemima did not deign to answer.

None of the various bibelots in the library were particularly delicate looking. They included a hunting knife with a golden stag's head as the handle. Both ends looked lethal. The knife reposed on a table entirely made up of twisted antler's horns. Above the table an enormous glass case, placed between two bookcases, contained a regal stuffed salmon, swimming amidst some brilliant reeds. The label beneath it read: 'Caught by HRH Prince Charles Edward Stuart (HM King Charles III) off Eilean Fas...' Jemima recalled the jolly note struck in Charles Beauregard's original letter, 'My mother's doing...'

'Mummy caught that herself,' volunteered Clementina. 'On the home beat. She told me.' Clearly her concentration had not gone entirely. 'That's why she never put it in her book about BPC. Because it wasn't true. She didn't pretend the rose garden was planted by BPC or Sighing Marjorie either, like some people. She was very serious about her history.'

Jemima shot another stealthy look at the stag's-head knife.

'I've never seen this famous white rose garden.'

'Red rose garden.' Clementina glared at her. Jemima cursed herself. Clementina's moment of weakness—or intelligence—had passed.

'Where the hell's the champagne?' she cried petulantly. 'Hasn't Duncan come back with it yet?'

'Not with the Chief on his way!' exclaimed Lachlan in a shocked voice. 'It would never do for him to find us drinking at this hour of the morning. You know how strong he is against the drink.' The Puritanism was unexpected: she wondered again who the Chief might be, and whether she might get to glimpse him. His identity was doubly intriguing now that the display of guns, the abduction of Colonel Henry, the detention of Ben and herself, had rudely jolted her complacency concerning the Red Rose. She was obliged to take them seriously as a force: it was no longer possible to dismiss them as a mildly eccentric but fundamentally harmless bunch of royalist fanatics.

After a while Clementina began to wander round the library again. She played some more music, loud, aimless. The champagne did not arrive. Nor for that matter did anyone else. Jemima considered it her duty to edge in the direction of the knife. Lachlan, showing signs of nervousness, put down his gun and demanded a cigarette from Clementina. She tossed him one out of her woven handbag. It was presumably an ordinary cigarette.

The time passed very slowly, according to the ornate golden clock, French perhaps, supported by rampant stags in baroque attitudes, on the heavily carved mantelpiece.

'I could do with a dram myself,' observed Lachlan wistfully after a while. 'Chief or no Chief. I'm no too fond of the champagne, you understand.' He sounded apologetic.

'You drank enough of it with Charles in the old days.' Clementina was cross.

'I was preferring the ancient whisky, though. The great old barrel.'

'You certainly were. I've never seen anyone as drunk as Lachlan on our last birthday. It's extraordinary stuff. Dark brown. Lays people out like flies. One hundred and twenty percent proof, or a thousand and twenty percent proof, something like that. Over a hundred years old, Uncle Henry told us. He nearly had a fit when we started to lay into it, the moment Charles was twenty-one, and slosh it about to the ghillies and Lachlan and other good souls like him.'

At very long last—they had surely waited much longer

than an hour—the noise of a car was heard. Distant at first, then growing stronger as it puttered up the valley.

Clementina gave a surprised little cry and stepped back from the window.

'Oh, it's not him. It's—' Lachlan sat up sharply, threw down his cigarette and grabbed the gun. In the split second his attention was diverted, Jemima made a dive for the knife with the stag's-head handle and stuffed it down her boot. She blessed the fashion for wide-cuffed cowboy boots. It felt uncomfortable, but safe.

'How *weird*! Where's the Chief, then?' Clementina sounded genuinely puzzled. The noise of the car grew louder and Jemima reckoned from the bumping, grating sound that it was just crossing the drawbridge; then the most extraordinary sound of singing from downstairs greeted her ears, followed by running footsteps and cries, mixed with protests and more snatches of a very drunken, very Scottish song which as it grew nearer sounded increasingly obscene. Then Aeneas burst into the library, hauling Duncan by his collar. The old man was still trying to sing.

'He's got out,' he panted. 'The devil. He's gone. Bribed him with the whisky and went.'

'It wasn't the drink at all, so it wasn't. It was the paper. We was just celebrating the paper.' As the tears coursed down Duncan's cheeks, he held out a crumpled piece of paper.

'You drivelling old fool,' snarled Aeneas, shaking the old man by his collar. 'What good will this paper do you? Do you think the laird will honour that?'

'He's promised me the lodge. The colonel would'na break his word. He's a man of honour.'

'He'll break you more like,' commented Lachlan. 'You'll never stay on the Estate now. Not now you've tried to force the Colonel to sign that paper.'

As an expression of maudlin horror and dismay crossed

Duncan's features, Jemima saw her chance. The library door was open. She pelted out of it, slamming it behind her. A vast key, shining and brassy like everything at Castle Beauregard, rattled in the lock as she did so. She turned it. It worked. The lock clicked fast as frantic shouts from the three men trapped inside reached her together with, a moment later, the strong rattling of the door itself. But the door held. Thank God for Leonie Beauregard who had refurbished the Castle in such a splendidly robust style. No rusty keys in locks here.

Jemima ran as fast as she could down the broad stairs to the arched entrance to the dungeon, scrabbling and hobbling in order to remove the stag's-head knife from her boot as she did so. At that moment the sound of other voices, urgently talking—in the armoury, or at any rate inside the Castle—reached her. The unknown visitor—the Chief or another—was within. Jemima was taking no chances. She shrank behind the arch and began to creep as quietly as possible down the stairs.

Footsteps, it sounded like a single man, went past her and right on up the main staircase. Let the unknown, whoever it was, cope with the imprisoned men and Queen Clementina. She had not dared to pause long enough to remove the key from the lock. It was up to her now to find Ben Beauregard.

Dungeons? There was now a maze of new staircases facing her below the level of the ground. But her task was made unexpectedly easy by the mint-new condition of even the subterranean regions of this castle. There were actually notices in Victorian Gothic directing her. TO THE CELLARS—she found herself by the entrance to a large room, vast in style, door open, clean, white-washed, vaulted. Not only the racks of bottles but the stink of whisky emanating from an outsize barrel convinced her that here had been Duncan's downfall.

Then she heard a noise behind her. She stopped. The noise stopped too. Someone was following her. Heart thumping, Jemima wondered why, if her pursuer were a member of the Red Rose, he did not immediately brutally grab her. She started to walk on gingerly, extremely gingerly, in the direction indicated for the dungeons. There was no sign of a guard or sentry. Had they left Ben quite unguarded in the furore of his father's escape and the unknown's arrival?

Another stealthy noise behind her. She tested it by stopping. But her follower was quick to follow suit. As Jemima proceeded along the narrowing passage, it was like playing an elaborate game of mediaeval grandmother's footsteps. Then she saw the dungeon—clearly labelled. The door was open. A body—Ben—was slumped in one corner. The ropes were wound round it. He looked horribly inert.

She gave a little cry and tried too late to stifle it. Then a strong muscular arm reached her from behind and stifled her voice completely. Jemima tried to scream and could not: then she struggled in earnest.

'Keep still, darling,' said a voice in her ear. 'I told you I'd be back. I didn't expect *you* to come looking for *me*.'

At the same moment as Jemima recognized the voice, deep even in its low tones, she also felt a wave of violent recognition for the physical touch of Henry Beauregard.

'Ben,' she mouthed.

'Shh,' he said, not letting her go. 'It's only the dummy. Ben's got away.'

Jemima felt her body relax. She realized how corpse-like the body in the dungeon looked to her. First the father, then the son . . . The dummy had a lot to answer for. The Colonel took his hand from her mouth and kissed her. It was done with a certain carelessness, as one might kiss a child who has been soothed.

'You poor darling,' he said gently, stroking her cheek, and pushing back the hair which had fallen over her face.

'Ben's gone to get help?' asked Jemima, still panting slightly from her journey, her fright and now the reassuring kiss at the end of it all.

'Help? I *am* help, aren't I?'

'I mean, *help*; proper help. The Red Rose, I mean, aren't you going to do anything about them—they kidnapped you.'

'For God's sake, girl, I am doing something about them!' exclaimed the Colonel, his voice getting louder as he struck a note of real indignation.

'What about the police? You must send for the police. First they kidnapped you, then they locked you up. They locked us up. Besides, they've got guns, they were firing shots over the Land-Rover.'

'They didn't kidnap me, as a matter of fact. There was a signal outside the window. A kind of whistle: family signal, something we use out in the woods. I don't know how they found it out. You were asleep. I left that note and went downstairs. And they jumped me. Three against one. As for the police, these are the sort of blackguards who simply need a good thrashing from some of my stronger ghillies,' he responded robustly.

'The guns—' began Jemima again. He ignored her.

'Besides, it didn't take me very long to outwit them. Duncan never has had a head for drink. None of his family can take it.'

'And you promised him the lodge. For ever. And he believed you.'

'All part of his general idiocy when he's had a drop. As if I'd ever give him the Old Lodge—we need the lodge. He knows that perfectly well: it's right in the heart of the Glen. He can whistle for his lodge. The old fool.' The

Colonel sounded almost as contemptuous as Aeneas had done.

'But you're not going to sack him?'

The Colonel looked at her as if she were insane.

'Sack Duncan Stuart? But he's worked on the Estate all his life. Besides, his son's a rotten type. Have to look after poor old Duncan, y'know. Can't go sacking him at his age.'

'His son—'

'Aeneas Stuart. Red-haired bastard—in every sense of the word. You must have seen him. He's the one who's really behind the Red Rose up here. Too clever by half. A real Red. Went to Aberdeen University and came back with a lot of half-baked ideas about land for the people, and knew less about the land and farming round here than his own grandfather who was an illiterate crofter. Not Duncan's fault: no brains to speak of there. The brains came from his mother Ishbel who was head housemaid before the war: wonderful head on her shoulders, but always causing trouble with the rest of the servants. You know the type: we never could keep a cook when she was around. Eleven cooks in one year, till we sacked Ishbel. You've probably been through the same thing yourself.'

Jemima had not.

'Trouble-makers have to go,' went on the Colonel. 'Same thing with Aeneas. Talk about the perils of educating people above their station. In the end I had him thrown off the Estate, told Duncan I wouldn't have him up the Glen. Suggested the Army, but of course he wouldn't go. Then my precious nephew Charles, he brought him back to spite me.'

'And you're still not going to take any official action?'

'In my own glen,' replied the Colonel grimly, 'I am the official action. This is between the Red Rose and me. No outside interference. Round One to them. Round Two to me.'

In short, to her utter amazement and, it has to be said, considerable dismay, Jemima found that the Colonel had worked out a plan by which they would now both leave the Castle together, as Ben had done, via the ruins of Castle Tamh. At which point the Colonel would joyously put into effect his proposals for defeating the Red Rose by his so-called 'official action'—it had exactly the opposite sound to Jemima—while she herself struggled back to the Wild Island on foot.

'Meet you there later,' said the Colonel. 'I'll be in touch.' He might have been discussing a London rendez-vous, such was his insouciance.

Jemima was torn between admiration for his spirit and a gloomy presentiment, the product of an innately law-abiding nature, that it would be both better and safer in the long run to hand over the Red Rose, Clementina Beauregard and all, to the Inverness-shire police. Let them iron out exactly what charges covered the somewhat strange circumstances; assault, the use of an offensive weapon, they would certainly not lack for material.

But Jemima found that her own sense of propriety and law and order was no match for the Colonel's sense of adventure and challenge. He was quite determined not to be personally done down by the Red Rose: indeed he hardly listened to her arguments concerning the police, which he seemed to regard as charmingly feminine—and as such deserving a reassuring caress rather than any more serious consideration.

Jemima gave up. In England, she knew, she would not have given up. She was not in England.

Meekly, she followed the Colonel through a maze of corridors in the well-dusted dungeons.

'Played in them as a boy with Carlo. Know more about

this castle than the Red Rose ever will,' he said by way of explanation.

The little arched side door by which they eventually left the Castle was swinging open, giving a broad path of light. Ben had left it open. As they approached the door, Jemima caught her breath: framed in the stone arch was an extraordinary vision of crimson, a great slope of roses, slipping away from her eyes towards the loch, like some field of poppies in the violence and concentration of its colour. She was seeing for the first time the famous Beauregard rose garden.

She ducked and stepped into daylight. They were among the ruins of the old castle, once again neatly finished off with new masonry, and adorned here and there with wooden identifying tags in the grass: The Great Hall, The Chapel, and so forth. The stone was grey, like Eilean Fas, in contrast to the dark red brick of the nineteenth-century edifice behind them, and the crimson roses which lay ahead.

The beds of flowers stretched almost as far as the loch, which curved round to meet the Castle on this side; but the garden itself was sheltered from both the wind and the view, which explained why she had never before glimpsed this monstrosity either from the road or the castle library. For monstrosity it was: seeing what must once have been an exquisite grey and white vista transformed into a fiery demonstration of family hatred made Jemima understand for the first time the nature of Colonel Henry's personal outrage against his nephew and his followers.

She kept these thoughts to herself. She felt the Colonel needed no encouragement in his feud.

They parted at the side of the loch, still hidden from view from the Castle. Equally Jemima could not see the courtyard, nor whose car it was which had arrived at the

Castle while she was in the dungeons—assuming she would have recognized it.

As she tramped, wearily but curiously elated, along the road which led down to the Eilean Fas bridge, she thought about cars and how sometimes, though not always, they were significant expressions of the personality. Her own Volvo sports car expressed a passion for fast but safe driving, a recklessness which did not find many other expressions in her character—except possibly in the present instance in her submission to the adventurous plans of Colonel Henry, against the judgement of the cooler part of her nature.

She was meditating on this and allied topics concerning her nature and that of Colonel Henry, as she reached the narrow wooden-slatted bridge. The noise of the water was loud in her ears. She reached out for the sagging rope which served as a handrail.

It was only at that moment that she became aware, quite suddenly, that a car had come up right behind her, was in fact touching her with its bumper nudging at her—the rushing of the water had totally masked its silent approach. Jemima stepped instinctively sideways to get out of its way, nearly slipping off the wet bridge as she did so. She clutched once more at the rope, for a moment swaying perilously over the water, fighting for her balance.

'Why, my dear Jemima,' said the drawling voice of Ossian Lucas. 'I hope I didn't startle you. I was just coming to pay my respects. Don't look so frightened.'

SIXTEEN

Appearances

The last stretch of the journey up to the Wild Island, in Ossian Lucas's car, was a silent one. Neither the MP (wearing velvet trousers and an extravagant silk shirt, patterned with lilies) nor his passenger had anything to say. Jemima Shore, as she watched his strong hand in its fanciful cuff on the driving-wheel, was glad to leave the rickety bridge behind.

She looked back at the black waters as the car climbed the winding gravel path—waters which had already claimed two victims in the shape of Charles Beauregard and Bridie Stuart and might even just now have claimed her. After her recent experiences, she badly needed a sense of security, protection; she wasn't quite sure whether the presence of the enigmatic Lucas provided it.

As if in answer to a prayer—an analogy which seemed peculiarly apt under the circumstances—there was a letter waiting for her on the stained and cracked hall table. She did not know what agency had brought it here, but since the house had been generally tidied, she imagined wearily that since life must go on in the Highlands, some substitute for Bridie had been found.

Jemima recognized the neat precise handwriting and thin, cheap paper immediately. There were the initials A.M.D.G.—*ad majorem Dei Gloriam:* To the Greater Glory of God—in the corner. Mother Agnes had written from her convent, that ivory tower from which she saw so many things so much clearer than ordinary mortals.

'Excuse me,' she burst out impulsively to Ossian Lucas. 'I must read this—a very valued friend—a nun as a matter of fact. A really good woman. Then I'll find you a drink; only wine, I'm afraid.'

But as they proceeded into the drawing room, a quarter of a bottle of malt whisky, neatly placed beside two clean glasses, contradicted her words: Colonel Henry's residue. Ossian Lucas helped himself, a dram, no water at all, and drained it.

Jemima was busy scanning her letter. It was extraordinary; one of these days she would really have to accept the powers of divine inspiration. Or rather, one of these days she would really have to examine the whole subject of religion seriously, i.e. *not* from the point of view of television programmes... As she had once told Mother Agnes, only half joking: 'I never seem to get time to think about God. It's all right for Him—if He exists—He's got all the time in the world.'

Mother Agnes had merely smiled politely.

Divinely inspired or not, Mother Agnes's present letter showed an extraordinary percipience about the situation in Glen Bronnack, although she had no means of knowing how much of dramatic import had taken place since Jemima wrote her letter recounting a tale of two brothers.

On the subject of the family:

... At its best an incarnation of the highest principles of human conduct, a source of wonderful comfort. Yet isn't it distressing how the Devil will never leave even the most sacred institutions alone? He is so determined to spoil things, if he can. Members of the family are also subject to special temptations of jealousy towards each other. Remember Cain and Abel, Jacob and Esau in the Old Testament. Passions so often run high in big families; such feelings are of course intended by Almighty God for the preservation and protection of His ordained unit, the family, but in certain cases, as with all human passions, the instinct, being perverted, can go awry. It can be turned towards evil. Sometimes I think Our Blessed Lord tests a pair of brothers with special temptations. He Himself of course was an only child...

It was Jemima's turn to smile at the last sentence.

'Christ,' said Ossian Lucas suddenly, interrupting her thoughts. 'I hate this house. I don't understand how you can stay here, and alone. There is such a feeling of sadness about it. A sort of doom hangs over it.'

'More than sadness: menace, threat,' responded Jemima.

'Then you feel it too. You didn't say.'

'You are the first person who has mentioned it to me.'

'An unhappy woman. Maybe she haunts it now, poor soul. God rest her too.' He poured and drank another dram of whisky.

'Sighing Marjorie?'

Ossian Lucas looked surprised. 'That's a long time ago. I meant poor Leonie Beauregard.'

'What?'

'Didn't you know? She committed suicide in this very house. Upstairs. When the twins were about twelve or thirteen. Shot herself with one of the guns from the Beauregard Armoury. A shotgun: an appalling death for a pretty woman. The worst of it was that Charles found her. It was no wonder that the poor boy turned odd as he did. And they left this house to rot. That's why Father Flanagan has always wanted to take it over for the Church—put matters right, in his not so humble opinion. As you may or may not know, and it's of absolutely no relevance now, our Henry and his beautiful American sister-in-law were not unattached in those far-off days. Father Flanagan first tried to persuade Charles himself to found the mission ostensibly in memory of his father; but of course for Charles the experience of being tutored by the turbulent priest was enough to lay the foundations of a most sincerely felt dislike for him and all he stood for. Seeing as he had a hatred of authority in any form, and Father F. seemed a particularly large and grim embodiment of it.

'Now Father F. is going on at Henry about it, but Henry knows how to deal with him all right. He replies most smoothly that if he had Clementina's money, coupled with the Beauregard land, he would be only too delighted to found a mission; as it is, with large estates to handle, a vast family, and not a great abundance of cash, it's out of the question for the time being. One day perhaps . . .'

'Is he sincere?' asked Jemima curiously.

Ossian roared with laughter.

'Absolutely not. Frankly, now he's managed to inherit it all, I can't imagine Henry handing over anything, let alone an island in the middle of the Estate. But the point is that Father Flanagan is kept quiet and the old dragon keeps hoping and waiting without too many sermons on the subject of sin and expiation in Henry's unwilling ear.'

A sort of doom hangs over it: his phrase echoed in her mind. There was certainly a sort of doom over Eilean Fas, with violent death polluting her Paradise down the ages from Sighing Marjorie and her baby to the widowed Leonie Beauregard two hundred years later.

Not a lucky house: the words of Mother Agnes suddenly appeared more relevant. Passions intended by nature for the preservation of the family had indeed in this case turned to evil, the evil of self-destruction.

Had the suicide been on account of Henry Beauregard? In that case it was no wonder that the twins had grown up to hate and resent him.

Jemima tried to tell herself that the house no longer felt evil to her, only tragic, now that she knew its secret. But she was happy all the same to accept Ossian's invitation for a stroll round the island, out into the mellow sunlight, the dancing yellows and greens of the afternoon.

'The land, the island,' said Jemima at one point. 'How obsessed you all are with the island.'

'Land equals the lure of gold in a primitive community. Are you surprised? Besides, it's our history. It's difficult to understand from outside. Take a previous tenant of Eilean Fas, in a manner of speaking—Bonnie Prince Charlie. Did he really come to rescue the people of Scotland from English thralldom? Or did he come to set up yet another form of dominion? Admittedly Catholic where the Hanoverians were Protestants, but since not everyone in Scotland is or was a Catholic by a long chalk, he could have represented slavery too.'

'I suppose he represented independence,' suggested Jemima hopefully; once again she cursed her English ignorance of Scottish history.

'Wouldn't true independence have been represented by setting up an independent kingdom of Scotland? Ignoring the English throne for better or for worse. As King James the Sixth and First might perhaps have ignored the throne of Elizabeth, and his mother Mary too.'

It was the most beautiful clear day she had yet experienced on the island. The misty beginnings, during which she had, as it were, stormed the castle perilous, had given way to unusual heat. The dampness of the undergrowth still exuded a jungle atmosphere. The cliffs fell away beneath them through the frondy bracken and other foliage. Her island Paradise was once more in evidence. Yet glancing at Ossian's face beside her, in profile strong, even goat-like above the striking silk shirt and purple trousers, she thought how little she knew of this stranger. How little she knew of any of them in this part of the world, a primitive community as the MP had said, obsessed by so many things: land and inheritance and history and a view of the past and the future which she did not understand.

'You don't take that point of view, surely,' Jemima countered. 'You're a democratically elected representative, for a Scottish constituency, sitting in an English Parliament.'

Ossian Lucas smiled: the satyr-like impression was enhanced and then faded.

'British Parliament,' he corrected her.

'But you don't share the wish for independence—' she persisted.

'You have to see all the sides of the question when you are a Scottish MP. If you want to survive. It's called the pragmatic approach. Come, let's look at the Fair Falls.'

The torrents of water dashed away from beneath their feet like a suicide's desperate jump. Sunlight played on the corner of Marjorie's Pool: they could both hear the high mourning sound of the water in the rocks, the voice of the Prince's lost love.

'You're very brave to come here among us like this,' said Ossian suddenly. He spoke in a low voice, but she could still hear him above the waters. 'Aren't you afraid of the passions you might stir up? As that waterfall stirs the dark waters of Marjorie's Pool.'

'There were passions enough before my arrival.'

'True enough. But perhaps there was a kind of balance, evenly matched forces—' He broke off. 'Jemima, I don't want to say more at the present time, but I do want you to be very careful whom you trust. Even the best of us, the good ones, can come to believe that the end justifies the means. Things here are seldom all they seem. I have a feeling that, coming from your world of television, sophisticated as it may be, and don't forget I'm no stranger to it—' he smiled as though in pleased personal tribute to his own publicity-seeking image—'you may trust too much to appearances.

'Take our evening at Kilbronnack, the dinner party for the Princess. Perhaps you saw Colonel Henry only as the ideal of the handsome laird, Ben his dashing son, Rory the quiet good sort, Kim the charming young boy and so forth. Don't forget that the Glen has also brought forth the hysteria of Clementina Beauregard, the bitterness of Aeneas Stuart, to give only two obvious examples. If this were a television programme—and once again I'm by no means averse to these things—appearances would be everything. But we are far from television, are we not, in this particular closed-in valley? Besides, there is such a thing as the manipulation of appearances, is there not, even through the ever-truthful medium of television?'

He was teasing her. 'If you were to make a programme about me, for example—and don't let us rule it out for a minute by the way, the eve of the next election would suit me best, just outside the electoral period, suggested title 'The Tales of Ossian Lucas,' all aspects of Highland society— if you were to do that, do you not think I would manipulate my own appearance? Beginning but not ending with my wardrobe, I should certainly try.'

'And I should certainly try to stop you,' replied Jemima with spirit. Still, 'The Tales of Ossian Lucas' was not to be rejected totally; it might be nice to get something positive out of her Highland holiday, weird experience as it had turned out to be.

Ossian Lucas had become serious again.

'I warn you: there's something going on in this glen, something dark and primitive working itself out. I'm not even sure about it myself yet. You could be hurt. Come, let's see the shrine.'

He took her arm and gave a light push. Jemima gasped. Ossian immediately steadied her. 'You see what I mean? You too could be hurt as Charles was and Bridie was. You nearly slipped on the bridge just now. Be careful. Watch your step.' His words gave an extraordinarily sinister impression. 'Go back to London,' he said, 'before it's too late.'

Then they walked in silence down the soft path to the shrine. Something red and fiery glowed there through the Gothic windows. Jemima stepped inside. Beneath the shrine to Charlotte Clementina Stuart was a bunch, an enormous bunch, of blooming red roses.

She touched the petals, damp and velvety.

'Why, they're quite fresh,' she said in a startled voice.

'So they should be,' Ossian's voice came from directly behind her. She turned round. His figure filled the doorway, another pattern of red against the bright light.

'I only put them there this morning. The dew was still on them. Don't you like red roses?' His tone was mocking.

'Not particularly, as it happens.' She added, 'And it seems rather an inappropriate gesture to come from you.'

'Oh, do you think so?'

'Don't you?'

'Hardly. As a loyal member of the Red Rose, I find it very appropriate indeed.'

There was a long silence between them.

'I warned you, Jemima Shore, things up here are seldom all they seem,' said Ossian Lucas at length.

'I was beginning to guess,' she began in rather a faint voice. 'Your appearance just now. So timely. I'll alter my charge. I find you a very inappropriate member of the Red Rose.'

'Why so?' Against the light she could scarcely discern his face above its frilly shirt, but she suspected that his lips were still curving in that Pan-like smile. The long narrow bony face and curly fair hair were hidden. 'The local MP and all that. Why, you're not even from these parts!' she exclaimed. In her nervousness, she was aware that she had uttered two contradictory statements. 'Where *are* you from?' she demanded in her most brusque interviewing manner. 'You really can't get away with having "mysterious origins" in this day and age.'

'Jemima Shore, Investigator, is back, I see,' commented Ossian. He was quick to see and mimic her change of manner.

'My dear girl,' he went on, most blandly, 'but of course you're quite right. My origins are not particularly mysterious to me—though I may choose to present them as such to the rest of the world. If I told you—with perfect truth—that I, not Henry Beauregard, was the real descendant of Sighing Marjorie and Bonnie Prince Charlie, would you find me an appropriate member of the Red Rose then?'

'The baby,' stammered Jemima, 'drowned in the river by the soldiers. Or rescued and brought up to marry a Beauregard.'

'Neither,' said Ossian. 'Nonsense—both stories. A child there was, a daughter Mary, as a matter of fact, brought up not far from here by foster parents and married later to a man called Lucas. I have the documents to prove it by the way, if I so wished. But for the time being I don't.'

'But Charlotte Clementina—the memorial on the island— she couldn't have been *invented*.'

'Oh, she existed all right. There was no need to invent her. A Stuart cousin, orphaned at Culloden as so many were, brought up by her relations—where was the drama in that? She may even have been the Prince's god-daughter, hence the choice of names. She existed all right in the Beauregard family tree.

'Her father was a Stuart, probably Marjorie's cousin, since everyone's related up here, but there is no direct connection with Eilean Fas. Getting back to my Mary Lucas who really did have royal blood—she was of course illegitimate. The marriage story is equal nonsense. Can you imagine a Prince in desperate straits bothering to marry some obscure Scottish girl? About the only chance left to him was to make some rich and grand continental marriage.'

'Then the Beauregards—how on earth did they get the idea?' Jemima felt herself to be quite bewildered. The folly, the legend, the claims of the Red Rose, where did it all fit in?

'The answer to that, my dear,' said Ossian Lucas with a laugh, 'is really quite simple. A mixture of two common Highland failings of the past, self-aggrandizement and self-deception. I'm not sure they could even be described as failings at a time when life was so hard hereabouts that survival at any price was the local motto. Plus a strong dose of American romanticism in our own day, to provide the finishing touches to the mixture.

'You see, for a long while after Culloden and the '45, everything round here was in complete chaos, with puni-tive government measures, estates forfeited and all the rest of it. Somehow, towards the end of the eighteenth centu-ry, when times got better, the Beauregards emerged not only with Castle Tamh and a good deal of the Glen restored to them, and Kilbronnack House which they owned already, but also Eilean Fas, the missing part of the

Glen. It rounded off the property and they had long coveted it. In the nineteenth century, a more orderly period, it was necessary to explain exactly how this had come about and the answer was simple: Charlotte Clementina Stuart must obviously have been the Eilean Fas heiress. And that made her the missing daughter of Sighing Marjorie, and that gave the Beauregards royal blood as well as a proper claim to the island. The royal blood side of it was all very vague and pleasant and word-of-mouth to the Victorian Beauregards: they gave their children Stuart names like Charles Edward and Henry Benedict, but the property was what mattered.

'And then of course Leonie Beauregard came along and in one of her mad fits of enthusiastic refurbishment and sorting out and clarifying, which she applied to the whole Castle and the Estates, decided to get the whole thing down between hard covers. Including her own ingenious— or perhaps ingenuous would have been a better word— theory of the marriage, which had certainly never been mentioned before. She it was who put up this folly, copied in the original style of the house, and the plaques. Naturally the story of the marriage was meat and drink to the Red Rose: provided them with a proper monarch of their own, right here in Glen Bronnack. In a way I rather admire the taste for fantasy in them all, from the Victorian Beauregards' clever legalization down to Charles Beauregard's exotic pretensions to be King of Scotland. Without, I'm afraid, being able to share it.' He looked down at himself, the velvet trousers whose hem was now bedraggled with grass and dew. 'My clothes express my only taste for fantasy. I prefer it that way.'

'But that changes everything!' cried Jemima. She suddenly realized that Ossian even looked quite like his royal ancestor, a less handsome but also a less effeminate version. It was the resemblance which had teased her in the drawing room of Kilbronnack House that night before dinner, gazing at the portrait.

'Does it?' answered Ossian in his quizzical style. 'I find it changes absolutely nothing so far. Nothing about the state of Scotland, which is what happens to interest me. Of course,' he added, 'it is true that Eilean Fas actually belongs to me, as the only living descendant of Sighing Marjorie, not to the Beauregards. If I chose to claim it, that is.'

SEVENTEEN

Remember Me

As Ossian and Jemima walked slowly back up the path towards the house, there was a violent thrashing in the undergrowth beside them.

Jemima screamed and clutched Ossian's arm. Then she regretted it: there were too many shocks, that was all. A deer, small, graceful, with little pointed ears and antlers, leaped across the path just in front of them.

'A roe,' said Ossian briefly. 'I wonder who or what put it up.' He did not seem surprised.

'Colonel Henry tried to kill one my first day here,' said Jemima more calmly than she felt. 'He told me they ate the tops of the young trees.'

'But there are no young trees at Eilean Fas, except the self-seeded ones,' replied Ossian. 'Nothing planted since Leonie Beauregard died here. Henry Beauregard just believes in extinguishing things which may get in his way for the principle of the thing.'

Jemima said nothing.

There was more noise among the leaves and bracken.

'Ah, so it was you,' continued Ossian. A dog bounded towards them, as though in very slow pursuit of the vanished deer.

It was Jacobite. As they came in sight of the house, a Land-Rover was seen to be standing there: Colonel Henry's.

'It seems that you have a caller,' said Lucas in an expressionless tone. 'I'll be off. I have a meeting tonight. No, not the Red Rose. My constituents: the above-board lot. They're really all my constituents of course. I shall discuss a Scottish assembly and all that sort of thing, wisely and sagely.'

'Is it wise to be quite so sure that I won't give you away?' she enquired. It was the first question she had asked him out there at the shrine: 'How do you know I won't give you away.'

'Two reasons, my dear.' He touched her cheek. There was something strong but sexless about his personality, as if his masculinity was held in abeyance by other stronger needs and interests.

'First, you're curious. An observer. A journalist. It's in your nature. You want to investigate mysteries—no, I'm not just punning on your series—you really do, I recognize it in you, above all you want to be in on things. Second, rather more practically, you have absolutely nothing to gain by so doing. I doubt if you could even prove it—I've kept my tracks pretty well covered, you may be sure, and Aeneas, Lachlan, and Co. would never give me away; even the Colonel himself, don't forget, begged you not to interfere between himself and the Red Rose.'

'Oh, that's his heroism,' said Jemima. '*Brother Raiders* and all that. I'm no heroine. You may do harm—' she began.

'We did you no harm. As a matter of fact we've never done anyone any harm.'

'Aren't you forgetting Hurricane Sophie?' she asked pointedly.

'Oh, that. Threats and counter-threats. A few slogans and counter-slogans. The brave little Princess, blue eyes popping, chin held high against the Highland fiends... That made everyone happy, including the *Daily Express* which gave it a headline. And of course as a publicity lover, it made HRH very happy indeed. I happen to know that she had no objection. There was never the remotest chance of action.'

'But they actually grabbed Colonel Henry, they tied up Ben—'

'Kidnapping Colonel Henry wasn't a bad idea except that they bungled it. One might have asked a ransom or at least got some nice anti-laird publicity. Tying up Ben was pointless and to involve you was ridiculous.'

'But will the Red Rose *never* do any harm?' she pressed him.

'I very much doubt it,' he said. The words were cynical, but Ossian Lucas sounded calm rather than cynical. 'Not the Red Rose itself: it's a gallant body of men, when all's said and done, just as gallant as the Beauregard brothers in their own way, romantics all, with their signs and signals and passwords and their Queen, and before that their King. The absurdity of it all,' he went on. 'Who wants to be a king? No, that's not where the power lies, in the empty shadow of royalty. What power did that little Princess have the other night? A minor royalty, a cousin of the monarch, daughter of a dunderhead duke, good for opening a dam or two, or closing down a regiment. Henry Beauregard, the laird, has more power up the Glen now that he's inherited it than HRH Princess Sophie of Cumberland has in the whole of Great Britain. That's why

I'm interested neither in my royal blood, nor in my claim to Eilean Fas. Neither can forward my own cause in the slightest.'

'Power is what interests you?'

'Precisely. True power. Not the myth of it, the outward show. As a member of the Red Rose I keep an eye on my most obstreperous constituents, consolidate my own position up here and whichever way the wind blows for Scotland in the future, why, I'm ready to blow with it. Either as the guerrilla turned statesman or the politician turned nationalist leader, depending on your point of view.'

'You're a wise man,' she said sarcastically. 'And a worthy Chief of the Red Rose.'

'Ah, my dear,' replied Ossian Lucas, adjusting his wide lily-patterned collar with perfect aplomb. 'You do me too much honour. I never for one moment said I was the Chief, did I? I am indubitably *not* the Chief of the Red Rose, as it happens. Now that really would be indiscreet. A nationalist leader in good time—yes. A guerrilla leader at the present time—no. But if you did know the identity of the present Chief, you would certainly understand for the first time, if I dare make the comment, how things really work in this part of the world.'

He would not be drawn further from this, to Jemima, both irritating and enigmatic remark.

'Oh no, my dear, I've sworn the most exotic oath, full of Gaelic words, of whose meaning frankly I didn't have the faintest idea. It would be most dangerous to break it under the circumstances; one might be turned into a toad, or even a crofter or something.' And from this maddeningly frivolous point of view he refused to budge.

In revenge, and to herself, Jemima wondered whether the genuine Red Rosers and their mysterious Chief were not more attractive than this ambivalent man—born losers as they might turn out to be. Ossian Lucas, as he had indicated, was a survivor. He could not, and therefore would not, lose.

Now, standing before the house, the MP prepared to jump into his own car with a wave through the window to the Colonel, but Henry Beauregard was gesticulating at him.

'We'd better go in then,' said Lucas. 'But don't forget what I said—'

'I won't betray you. Yet. Never fear. You're right. There's nothing to be gained, so long as the Red Rose steers clear of violence.'

'Oh, it's not *that*,' Ossian shrugged off his dual role— and who knew, maybe there were more—with indifference. 'Don't forget. Trust those least who are above suspicion. It's a good motto.'

Inside the house, Colonel Henry looked wonderfully spruce; he had all but finished his own bottle of malt whisky. He was wearing an immaculate dark suit of the kind which hung so well on his tall figure. His handsome silvered head was held high, chest thrust out. It was in fact the suit in which Jemima had first seen him—his funeral suit.

But on this occasion it proved to be his London suit. Henry Beauregard was off that evening on the overnight sleeper to London.

'Flying visit. Business meetings. Back in the morning. Sleepering both ways.'

'It's called doing a Colonel Henry in these parts,' observed Ossian *sotto voce*. 'He has lunch with his current lady friend, does his business and is back after two nights in a train looking a great deal fitter than you and me. He thinks Edith won't notice anything if he doesn't actually spend the night in London.'

To say that Jemima felt chagrin was a mild estimation of

her feelings. Wearily, she remembered that this was the man who had left her in the middle of the night for the lure of a family signal. Would it always be so? she wondered with childish disappointment; money, land, the island, the Glen, coming before... she stopped. She did not know how to finish the sentence. After all, what did she represent to Colonel Henry? She had not yet had even the briefest time to find out. A phrase from a long-buried programme, one of her first independent ventures, about South America, came back to her. Some handsome *gaucho* had told her that on the *pampas* the motto was '*Primero el cavallo, después la doña.*' First the horse, then the woman. In the Highlands, the same motto seemed to apply, roughly translated as: First the land, then the lady.

Jemima wondered if Colonel Henry had altogether forgotten that Saturday was her birthday, that he had promised to take her on an expedition—

'And I'll be able to buy a birthday present in London,' said Colonel Henry with a charming smile. 'That's really why I'm going. Nothing worthy of you in Kilbronnack.'

'There's always Robbie Mack's Tartan Shop,' suggested Ossian. 'The pride of Kilbronnack.' His voice was not without malice.

'On the contrary, I was thinking of Burlington Arcade.' And with that the Colonel dismissed the subject. In his usual slightly mocking manner, Ossian then made his farewells and left the island.

'What *about* the Red Rose?' she began as soon as he had gone. 'What about Clementina, the guns?'

'The Red Rose!' snorted Colonel Henry. 'We sorted them out pretty quickly, I can tell you. Sent over Jamie Mackay and the men. That soon sent them packing, vanished—the lot of them—at the hint of authority, just as they did at the church. I doubt if we shall see much more of Aeneas Stuart up here. Had the cheek to tell me

he had got some job in an American university as a
lecturer! Can you beat it? Damned Red. I've a good mind
to tip them off. I've still got a few contacts in the military
intelligence. At least it's not *our* money that's paying him.
Bloody fools, the Americans.'

Colonel Henry clearly derived some gloomy satisfaction
from the notion of Aeneas Stuart subsidized by a campus
in the United States.

'And Lachlan?'

'Ah, Lachlan. Going to work on the rigs, I hear. He'll
earn a fortune. But he'll be back one day, I'll be bound.
He was born in the Glen. He could never keep away long
from the Glen. Let that be. I've still got a score to settle
with Master Lachlan. Let him come back with his ridiculous Red Roses and see what kind of welcome he gets.'

Jemima thought that Lachlan probably would return;
but as Ossian had predicted, it would be under a new if
equally romantic banner, the Black Thistle, the Red Lion.
No doubt he would once again be defeated by Colonel
Henry—up Glen Bronnack at least.

She forbore to point out that by the same token Aeneas
too, son of Young Duncan and the housemaid Ishbel,
would be back one day to re-engage the Beauregards. She
was less certain about the outcome of that particular
struggle: but perhaps the next contest would turn out to be
between Aeneas and Lachlan.

'Their Chief,' she began uncertainly. 'They talked of
their Chief.'

'Oh, talk, talk,' Colonel Henry airily dismissed the
subject. 'Told my niece Clementina that if she didn't
behave herself I'd have her certified,' continued Colonel
Henry. 'Gave her a good fright. Then I left a couple of
men with her to stand guard and stop the Castle being
used in future as a refuge for those kind of ruffians. Edith'll
go over later and calm her down—woman's work—and all

that. Besides, old Edith has got to organize the move into the Castle sooner or later; she'll hate leaving Kilbronnack House no doubt after all these years, and her garden. Still,' he brightened, 'plenty of scope for gardening at the Castle. For one thing the rose garden. Get rid of those bloody red roses. Oh yes, Edith will be much too busy to mope.'

Poor garden-loving, mope-forbidden Edith, thought Jemima, but the Colonel was still pursuing his own line of thought.

'No, we shall hear no more of the Red Rose in these parts, I can assure you.' He sounded extraordinarily confident.

'Look—on your birthday, I thought we might have a picnic for you, here at Eilean Fas, with Edith and the boys, and then a sort of private stalk afterwards. It's a game we used to play when they were small. Stalking round the island. Someone suggested we should do it again. Father Flanagan, as a matter of fact, put it to Edith. It turns out August 30th *is* her birthday. Wouldn't that be jolly?'

'Awfully jolly,' said Jemima in her most polite voice.

'I'll get Ossian, even ask Clementina. Heal the breach. Good idea? Blood is thicker than water and so forth.' There was a vague quality of embarrassment about his remarks. Jemima suspected the influence of Father Flanagan.

And that, it seemed, was that.

The island became very quiet again while Colonel Henry was away. It returned to its feeling of Paradise. Although Jemima never quite got over her fear of the house. 'Rest, rest, perturbed spirit,' she thought of Leonie Beauregard. But the house still seemed to her melancholy, obscurely evil.

She wrote to Guthrie Carlyle in answer to a long letter from him, and found that she had nothing much to say except to thank him for feeding Colette in her absence.

She missed Colette and thought that it would be nice to enjoy her cool undemanding company at Eilean Fas; she no longer felt the same about Guthrie Carlyle.

She received three visits from Ben, Hamish and Kim Beauregard respectively. They came, with a nice sense of hierarchy which seemed appropriate to their family structure, in order of age.

Ben suggested wistfully once again that a programme about the Beauregard Estates ... He also suggested taking her out in London. Despite his good looks, Jemima remained non-committal. She felt that one Beauregard in her life— if indeed he was in her life and not rattling to and from in a sleeper 'doing a Colonel Henry'—was enough.

Hamish Beauregard did not suggest taking her out. He arrived with Jacobite. He was extremely polite but, like his appearance, his conversation was stolid rather than exciting. In fact the whole purpose of his visit was a little mysterious to her. He related various anecdotes—not in themselves very interesting to her—about pigeon-shooting with his brother Rory in the woods round Eilean Fas whenever both happened to be up in the Glen at the same time. It was only as he was leaving, and she was thanking him for his call, that he suddenly blurted out quite abruptly a remark about duty. Didn't she think it was difficult at times to know where one's duty lay? He was half inside the Land-Rover. It seemed a singularly inappropriate moment to discuss duty. His head bent over the steering wheel, he said:

'If one knew something, something horrible about someone one knew, a little thing, but it might be a big thing really, if one thought about it, the more one thought about it, the more one might wonder, one might think one ought to do something?' The 'ones' and 'someone' and Hamish's peculiar upper-class circumlocutory manner of expression made it almost impossible to understand what he was talking about; but it was possible to understand that he was worried, under strain. He ended quite abruptly with a simple question: 'How long have you known my cousin Clementina, Miss Shore?' then immediately and hastily brushed his own question aside and put the vehicle in gear.

'Why don't we talk?' Jemima felt that it was her own duty to suggest at least that, despite her need to get back into the house, to be alone.

Hamish straightened up and smiled a sweet boyish smile.

'Oh, I'm probably imagining things,' he said. 'Pure imagination. I don't know why I'm going on like this.'

But after he left, Jemima reflected that he did not seem to her the sort of person who would easily imagine things. Long afterwards she wished she had pressed Hamish Beauregard further at just that tiny instant of his weakness, and not allowed her own selfish desire for solitude once again to prevail, to permit his departure.

Kim Beauregard's visit was altogether more pleasant and straightforward. For one thing he proved the most tremendous chatterbox. He arrived on his bicycle and left half an hour later having eaten and drunk most of the supplies in the house, without ceasing to talk except to take an occasional breath between food and gossip. The sulky teenager in his jabot of the royal dinner party was quite absent. Jemima learnt a great deal from Kim, including the nature of the projected private stalk on Saturday.

'It's a game we play on Mum's birthday. Father Flanagan invented it. Stalking Dad,' he explained. 'Otherwise known as the Getaway, getting away from Mum, that is, with all her fussing over the picnic things and food and not getting Dad into too much of a bait and us not drowning ourselves and shooting ourselves. It's terrific: this is the first year we've been allowed to play it on Eilean Fas—oh, since

Aunt Leonie did herself in. You see she did herself in on a picnic. And cousin Charles found her. I wasn't born then of course, I'm known as The Afterthought, but Bridie told me about it afterwards.' Jemima shivered and quickly changed the subject.

Apart from that, life on Eilean Fas was calm; Father Flanagan, for example, could not exactly be classed as a visitor, since he paid no actual visit. But during an afternoon stroll to the Fair Falls Jemima did glimpse once again the tall black figure of the priest on the opposite bank as she had done during her first tour of the island.

Once again she had the impression that he was gazing covetously at the green and private territory. On this occasion he did not wave but turned away, the shape of his dark soutane gradually disappearing amidst the trees. The noise of the water drowned all other sounds and had the effect of making the odd little episode like something out of a silent film.

On Saturday morning Jemima had a fourth visitor in the shape of Colonel Henry himself. He arrived very early in the morning before she was awake and came straight upstairs.

She said, very sleepily, from the bed. 'What is it?' In her dream someone was calling her, time to dress, go to Megalith House, record the programme, time to get up, yet she was asleep.

'Your birthday present. As promised.'

'You?'

'And that's not all. Look.' She raised herself on one elbow. He had placed an enamel box in the shape of a heart on her pillow. She read the two words: *Remember Me.* The lettering was curly and held aloft on the lid by two cupids.

'Remember you,' she said some time later, when the room was once more scattered with masculine clothes thrown down in a way which she was beginning to think was actuated not so much by amorous passion as by the natural arrogance of one who was sure someone else would pick them up. 'Yes, I'll certainly remember you.'

Remember me. In this house Leonie Beauregard, his former mistress, had died. Did he remember her? There were so many memories here, around her, near her. For one instant the message, the pretty charming little birthday message painted on the enamel box, struck her as sinister.

'Will you remember *me*?' she asked fiercely.

'Till my dying day,' replied the Colonel. But he was already hunting around the room crossly for his clothes as though someone should really have come into the room and tidied them while he was in bed. 'Till my dying day. That's a promise.' His tone was debonair, preoccupied.

But his words did not reassure her. She felt the ghost of the past suddenly most present between them.

EIGHTEEN

Outdoor Manoeuvre

There were no rainbows on the Wild Island that day; Jemima had hoped for one on her birthday. There was no rain either: but the weather on the birthday picnic lost the brightness it had retained since morning at exactly the moment that Colonel Henry proposed a toast to Jemima in champagne.

There was one bottle. Previously the 'boys' had drunk beer, Colonel Henry whisky and Jemima and Ossian Lucas white wine. Now Colonel Henry distributed the champagne according to some clearly ordained notion of precedence. A full glass for Jemima, a full glass for himself, a full glass for Ossian, half a glass for Ben (the heir), for Clementina (a lady), correspondingly smaller amounts for the rest of his sons, down to a mere drop for Kim (with a frown from Rory). Nothing for Father Flanagan. Nothing for his wife.

'Edith does not drink.'

Lady Edith smiled apologetically as though this was in some way her fault. She was busy clearing away the remains of the cold grouse which, together with smoked salmon, had constituted the feast. The salmon, caught and smoked on the Estate, was very good indeed, much better than that presented in London by Guthrie. But the grouse had been despatched north by those sporting sons who were currently missing, from more productive moors than those pertaining to the Beauregards. Jemima was ticked off by Kim for feeding pieces of abandoned grouse to the dogs: it was apparently the wrong thing to do, because of the splintery nature of the bones. Otherwise the picnic itself had been without incident except for a suddenly erupting fight between Flora and Jacobite.

The language of dogs was incomprehensible to Jemima. One moment both animals, identically golden, were lying placidly. The next, hair risen on the scruff of the neck, they were growling and fighting, aiming literally at each other's throats (the old cliché was true). Jemima could only assume the dogs carried through the feud within the Beauregard family.

Colonel Henry separated them, coolly and rather crossly, with some well-aimed kicks, saying, 'Clementina, Edith, control your dogs.' He seemed to think their ferocious behaviour was nothing to do with him.

Now he repeated, draining the bottle of champagne into his own glass, 'Edith doesn't drink.'

'She *does*,' said Kim in a fierce voice, 'Mum does drink. Besides, it's her birthday. She ought to have some champagne.' He glared, not at his father but at Jemima as though she were in some way responsible for abrogating his mother's birthday. As usual, Lady Edith bent herself to hushing him. Colonel Henry said nothing. All the same, the moment for Jemima was spoiled, just as the weather had clouded and darkened.

'Rain?' Ben looked at Rory.

'More like the Haar will come up from the river.'

Clementina shivered. She was wearing a cheesecloth top, and the long patchwork skirt she had worn on the occasion of their first meeting. She wore no shoes. Her feet were white and small on the damp green grass. She looked extremely beautiful but fragile. When Ben put his kilt jacket round her shoulders, she did not object. After a bit she put it on, looking more delicate than ever, swallowed up in the rough tweed material.

'If the mist comes up, perhaps we should cancel the stalk,' suggested Lady Edith. 'You might all get lost.' Colonel Henry looked sharply at his wife, than at Jemima and smiled. He gave the impression that the idea of a mist or Haar on the island, in which people might lose themselves, was not totally unacceptable to him.

'Of course we must have the stalk!' cried Kim. 'The Haar will make it better, not worse. A ghostly figure will loom out of the mist and before you know where you are you'll be dead! Much more exciting.'

'Ugh, how horrible,' exclaimed Clementina.

'Oh, not really dead,' said Kim impatiently. 'Don't you remember the rules? *Named* dead: Clementina, I name you, you are dead.' He began to wave his hands in front of Clementina's face in a ghoulish manner.

'The position of Eilean Fas, lying in the river bed, means that you can get those incredible mists, quite local, during the warm weather; something to do with two bands of air meeting each other. They can last for days when the rest of the world, even the rest of the Glen, is bathed in sunshine,' Rory explained politely to Jemima.

'I always think the charm of our dear Scottish weather is its changeability,' Lady Edith threw in.

'It's true,' said Clementina, 'you can look out of the

windows of Castle Beauregard and find the Wild Island has quite vanished from one moment to the next.'

'I don't think we should stalk if it gets too thick,' Ossian Lucas spoke languidly but with conviction all the same. 'I agree with Lady Edith. It could be dangerous. Someone could blunder over the cliff edge.'

'Oh, nonsense. We've all been playing the game since childhood.' Ben sounded quite angry.

'Miss Shore hasn't,' said Rory.

'That she hasn't,' Father Flanagan threw in grimly. The inference of his remark was quite plain: Jemima was a stranger in their midst. Up till now the priest had maintained a somewhat grumpy silence throughout the picnic. His birthday present to Jemima, proffered with a fierce aside—'Ye may like to glance at this or again ye may not'—consisted of the current parish circular of St. Margaret's. It included a passage from the Bible which, by coincidence or otherwise, happened to be the story of the woman taken in adultery. Jemima had a feeling that Father Flanagan's own approach to such a situation would have smacked more of the Old Testament than the New.

'Exactly,' said Ossian Lucas. Jemima got the distinct impression that camps were forming: Ben was keen on the stalk; Rory not. Kim dead keen; Hamish, who had evidently recovered from his fit of neurosis earlier in the week, keen as mustard, judging from his sole sporting comment—'Jolly good fun if somebody does go over a cliff!' Lady Edith was increasingly and openly worried about the consequences to her brood; Father Flanagan, despite Lady Edith's plaints, had become obstinately for, as though determined to spite Jemima. Clementina Beauregard, who throughout the picnic had remained perfectly pleasant but passive, as though drained of all her frenzy by the recent events at the Castle, showed no signs of trying to make such a difficult decision. Ossian Lucas was positively against. But Colonel Henry was for, and in the end, as usual, it was his will which prevailed.

He explained the rules of the stalk briefly but lucidly. Looking at him standing over the picnic scene—they were on one of the neglected terraces below the house, quite near the river—Jemima thought that this was how he must have briefed his men in those far-off heroic days of *Brother Raiders*. The same notion struck Clementina, who came to life for the first time.

'Uncle Henry, you sound so military,' she giggled. Her voice had changed slightly, very slightly but perceptibly. Jemima, becoming alert to her moods, looked at the cigarette in her fingers; at some point she had swapped a Rothman's for the familiar small white stub.

Colonel Henry was to be the focus of the stalk, designated as the Prey. All those present were his stalkers. Like a stag, he was aiming for sanctuary, in this case sanctuary being the Gothic shrine at the other end of the island. He would set off shortly from the terrace, being given fifteen minutes to get away and conceal himself. In order to kill the Prey, the stalkers had to touch him, the conventional words being: 'Colonel Henry Beauregard, you are my Prey!' But they had to do this unobserved, since in this hunt at least the stag also had the right to turn on his attackers. Unlike the stalkers, the stag did not have to touch the kill. If the Prey merely spotted any of his stalkers and was able to name them correctly, then that stalker was held to be dead, killed by the stag.

'How long does it all last?' enquired Jemima.

'Ages,' answered Kim gleefully. He was definitely the most enthusiastic member of the stalking party.

'The Prey must reach sanctuary by dark. He has to make a run for it then, if he hasn't got there already,' explained Colonel Henry. 'I should explain that there's a fifty-yard radius round the shrine where the stalkers can't lurk and the Prey can't hide. Once he enters it, he has to belt for sanctuary. The stalkers have to stalk him properly, up hill and down dale—I can safely promise you a great deal of exercise.' He smiled at Jemima again. 'There are all sorts of dips and caves at the top of the island. You can get quite lost in the bracken too. I've every intention of hiding myself for a good long time.'

'We can't wait till dark in this weather,' Ossian spoke softly but firmly.

'We're guid Scots—the most of us. We'll not mind a drop of moisture', was Father Flanagan's typically gruff contribution. But he found no further support. Even Ben, an advocate of the stalk, joined in on the other side.

'Yes, Dad,' agreed Ben. 'It's much better if we have a fixed time.'

After some discussion and some slightly pettish flashing of his watch by Colonel Henry—'Is this accurate enough for you? Gift of my brother officers when I got married' —the time of six o'clock was agreed. Colonel Henry did not like the idea of the afternoon's sport being cut short. Nevertheless by six o'clock, if the Prey had failed to reach the shrine, victory was to be declared to the stalkers.

But already dark was coming in the form of a thickening of the atmosphere. The mist had begun to roll up from the river just as Rory had predicted. The swirling clouds, light at first, but deepening, were grey: the effect was deadening, depressing, shutting out light, and reducing the colours of the island itself. The many greens became one rather dank green. The glimpses of yellow and purple—the wild flowers—the occasional brilliant berry were no longer prominent without the sunshine to pick them out. The house's dark Gothic shape loomed above them, floating out of the mist.

Quite soon the river itself vanished from view; but you knew the river was there from the perpetual sound of running water, the noise which never ceased on the Wild Island, and higher up too you could hear the soft roar of the Fair Falls plunging into the pool where Sighing Marjorie had perished...

And Charles Beauregard.

Clementina. His sister—and his heiress. The warning; the mysterious Chief's warning: the girl's high voice repeating it from the telephone: 'I'm in danger, he says.' And Clementina was invited to Eilean Fas, taking part in the Beauregard family picnic for the first time in years. Wasn't it odd, after the incident of the Red Rose, how first Colonel Henry had genially invited her, then Ben had looked after her in such a courtly fashion? Clementina Beauregard, if she no longer owned the Castle in which she lived, was still an extremely rich young woman. Other words floated back: 'I'll give it all to the Red Rose... If I die without children, half the money goes to the next owner of the Beauregard Estates, Uncle Henry or Ben...' An appalling notion struck Jemima. Land itself was good, but land with money is better. Just who was the intended Prey of this delightful family game?

She dismissed it with horror at herself. But just as the stalkers began to move off, fifteen minutes after the Colonel's disappearance, his tall figure last seen striding away up the terraces into the mist, she heard Rory say urgently to someone beside him:

'You must stay close to Clementina. Don't lose her. Don't forget.' Jemima was not sure whether to be reassured or otherwise by this remark.

As the mist continued to thicken, she herself resolved very firmly if unadventurously to stay on the path and head in the general direction of the shrine. Let the young Beauregards scramble over the hill if they wished. As for stalking Colonel Henry, she had a strong inkling that he on the contrary would be stalking her.

Like their Prey, the stalkers vanished quickly. Afterwards Jemima would recall perfectly the exact order in which they left. Lady Edith, aided by a reluctant Kim, and followed by a now submissive Jacobite, left first to deposit the remnants of the picnic in the Land-Rover before setting off to join the stalk. They would go separately— Kim having brushed off Lady Edith's suggestion that they should stalk together for safety with a furious 'Oh, *Mum*.' Father Flanagan strode off too in the same general direction. Jemima personally felt relieved once the mist had swallowed up his tall black figure with its aureole of white hair. He had the air of a prophet going off into the wilderness—a prophet in a bad mood.

Hamish said, 'Dad mentioned going up the hill didn't he? I think I'll follow.'

'Please yourself,' said Rory. 'Knowing Dad, he'll try to trick us. He'll expect us to go up the hill, so he'll lurk close to the house until the last moment. Then he'll dash very fast, over the hill towards the shrine, in order to make it before the deadline. He'll take the rest of us by surprise, kill us from behind, so to speak. No, I'll stay down by the terraces near the house, somewhere in the bushes.'

He went off.

Ben, like Rory, voted for exploring the hill but suggested searching the far side, away from the main path, where the cliffs were steepest.

'I've a notion there's a small cave on the underhang... Worth a look.' He too set off, saying as he went, 'Coming, Clementina?' But she did not follow him, announcing her intention rather vaguely of going towards the Fair Falls 'because they are so pretty.'

Jemima was reminded briefly and nastily of Duncan's sons in *Macbeth*, dividing their ways for security after their father's death. But no death had yet taken place, had it? The Prey was still at large.

Jemima was left alone with Ossian Lucas. She half expected him to volunteer to stay with her. Instead he exclaimed, 'Henry and his absurd games! I'll just pad around and keep an eye on things.' And he too was gone.

Jemima was now aware that altogether it was not actually raining, the mist had brought a kind of dampness of its own into the air. Moist globules were forming on her face and clothes. She yearned for her Burberry and jeans. Her honey-coloured suède skirt and waistcoat were hopelessly impractical for a stalk. Nor did she fancy chancing her long suède boots, which she had not been able to resist displaying, in the island rough.

Of course it had been firmly laid down that the house itself was out of bounds to everyone.

'This is a bracing outdoor manoeuvre, not a damned house party,' Colonel Henry announced. 'No one goes into the house without my express permission.' Jemima had been amused: he had evidently forgotten that she was the house's official tenant. Then she found Colonel Henry looking at her. He gave her a faint smile and lifted his eyebrows. So the gallant Colonel intended the house, not the bracken, as their rendezvous. Well, why not? Feeling rather reckless—besides, she refused to spend three hours combing the hill for a human stag—Jemima gave him a nod. Then she found that both Kim and Rory were looking at her. Kim was glaring again; Jemima felt slightly embarrassed.

Now she slipped rather furtively into the house to change her clothes. The rhododendrons near the house did not stir. She was fairly sure no one had spotted her.

The mist was not lifting. From her bedroom window she could see that even the first of the terraces was lightly swathed in it. The course of the river bed had become marked by a thick belt of fog.

Jemima threw the honey-coloured suit on the bed and began to pull on a black polo-necked jersey as rapidly as possible. It was while the jersey was over her head that she heard—or thought she heard—the sound of someone else in the house. Once her head had emerged, and she was zipping up her jeans, she heard nothing more. Muffled in the wool, it was difficult to be precise exactly what sort of noise it had been: a door shutting or banging somewhere? The front door? It seemed to come from that area. Once again there was complete silence. She did not feel frightened: but her instinct told her quite strongly that she was not, or had not been, alone in the house.

Surely no one else had cheated? She decided to leave the house herself as soon as possible and honourably join the stalk. Then she found the note: it was scribbled and only just legible. 'See you here in half an hour? H.B.B.' So it had been him.

Her heart lightened. Jemima was about to leave the house once more to join the stalk, when another faint sound attracted her attention. This time it indubitably came from the back quarters of the house.

NINETEEN

The Prey

The back offices of Tigh Fas, if you could use such a house agent's term for them, were surprisingly extensive and even rambling. They lay beyond a communicating door which shut them off from the front area of the house. Besides the large old-fashioned kitchen with its temperamental Aga there were not one but two deserted pantries, with cracked brown wood surrounds to their sinks where now Formica would have been obligatory; a larder with a cooling grille to the outside world reminded Jemima equally of the pre-refrigerator age; finally there was another spacious room, furnished solely by a broken sofa out of which horsehair tumbled; this Bridie had described without batting an eyelid as 'the staff sitting room: a verra nice room indeed, getting all the afternoon sun.' Outside the back door there were a series of outhouses and sheds, some containing practical needs of the day like wood, some relics of the past like a child's bicycle and a pram without wheels.

To tell the truth, Jemima herself never penetrated much beyond the kitchen; she did not care for these forgotten service areas haunted not so much by people as by a vanished sybaritic way of life. Now she hesitated. It was possible that Colonel Henry, having deposited his note, had gone out the back way. Yet unless her imagination was playing tricks, she was fairly sure that some vague movement was still going on in the house.

Her curiosity got the better of her. She opened the communicating door slightly and listened. There was someone there—more than one person, for she could hear talking. So she was not the only member of the stalk to disobey Colonel Henry's instructions not to enter the house (other than the Prey himself). She would investigate; it was after all her house—rented.

Cautiously Jemima went towards the kitchen. It was empty. She was obliged to pad further down the corridor, until she was brought to an abrupt halt by the fact that the door of the so-called staff sitting room was open, and she could see inside.

Lachlan Stuart was standing there. He was wearing a thick jersey instead of the familiar T-shirt, with its flower stain. But he was holding an enormous bunch of roses of the most violent bright crimson in his arms. They must have been plucked from the castle garden. He was saying something about remembrance. He was not looking in Jemima's direction, but fixedly and rather angrily at someone else concealed from her view behind the door.

Jemima froze.

'Aye, I ken right well the Red Rose is no more,' he went on, his voice rising slightly. 'But someone must remember us; we must'na be forgotten. And seeing as she's from the television, she'll remember us. Not let the world forget us. Surely you don't want us forgotten, now: you're our Chief.'

There was a pause. Jemima could not hear what was said.

'You *were* our Chief, then! But to me and the others you're still our Chief,' countered Lachlan angrily.

There was some answer from the person hidden by the door, but Jemima could not hear it. Lachlan looked increasingly distressed and clutched the roses; but there was nevertheless an expression of reluctant obedience on his face. It reminded her of the incident at the funeral when he had been commanded to abandon the coffin. Finally he flung the roses furiously away and out of sight.

He muttered something which she could not hear and then said more strongly, 'I'll be off now, right. I'll be off to the rig. I know: I must'na be seen here now. Dinna worry, Chief, the Haar will cover me as I go.' He strode to the door. His hands were empty. He said defiantly and quite loudly into the room, 'Up the Red Rose! Captain Lachlan salutes the Chief,' sketched some gesture with his fist, and vanished out of the back door into the mist.

There was a movement inside the staff sitting room. Jemima suddenly and desperately felt that it was essential for her to know who the Chief of the Red Rose was—or rather had been. She had to see, and not be seen, to satisfy her own sense of completeness concerning the weird tale of the Red Rose.

She shrank back into the larder; the room was both dark and chilly, with no proper window, only its grille to the wooden bank outside. Footsteps approached, calm unhurried footsteps. Jemima peered through the crack of the wooden door; the former Chief of the Red Rose passed so near to her that she was afraid her breathing would be heard. But he did not look back.

She watched the tall figure of Rory Beauregard walk easily away down the corridor into the house beyond.

Immediately Rory was gone, Jemima tiptoed back into the staff sitting room and saw the abandoned roses on the floor. There was a white card attached to them. She picked it up and read: 'Farewell to Jemima Shore from the Red Rose. Remember us.' She dropped the card and left it lying with the flowers.

Then she sank onto the sofa with its broken springs.

Rory Beauregard. The quiet deep brother who travelled about mysteriously; Rory Beauregard, in his own way a second son just as his father had been. The second son, siding with his cousin against his elder brother as being the lesser of the two evils. The second son who would do anything to gain Eilean Fas and had presumably organized the Red Rose to that end. Land hunger or land passion once again lay at the heart of it all . . . As Ossian Lucas had said: If you knew who the Chief was and why, you would understand more about this part of the world than you do at the present time.

A vignette came to her: Rory Beauregard commanding Lachlan to abandon his plan for the coffin. The words of Lachlan, 'Mr. Rory . . .' Then he obeyed. Another vignette: Rory commanding his brother Kim to stop drinking, and Lachlan again at the Castle: 'You know how strong the Chief is against the drink.' Rory Beauregard: a silent determined man, determined not to stay in the secondary position to which he had been born.

The sofa's springs hurt her and reminded her that it was neither pleasant nor politic to remain inside the house. Time was passing. She would have to think about it all later; perhaps one day, with tact and circumspection, she could induce Rory to unbend and tell her everything. Now that really would be a programme worth making, even if he sat with his back to the camera, like a terrorist. In the meantime she really must join the stalk.

Jemima left by the back entrance of the house, as Lachlan had done, carefully inspecting the bushes surrounding it to make sure she was unobserved. She decided to set off down the path which led to the Fair Falls.

She knew that Clementina had gone that way because the girl had advertised the fact; Jemima might be able to keep an eye on her. It was true that it was also the most exposed route from the point of view of the stalker. There was no cover to the right of the path, where the hill began to ascend, only low scrub, and Jemima had no intention of cowering to the left, within dangerous reach of the cliff edge, even to avoid the Prey's piercing gaze. But she had every reason to suppose that the Prey would not 'name' her and thus 'kill' her even if he did see her. The Prey was expecting her, alive and well, back at Tigh Fas in the not too distant future. He had no reason to draw attention to her whereabouts.

She proceeded, as discreetly as possible, along the crunchy gravel path and turned down the silent mossy track which followed the contour of the island. How different the Wild Island looked now from that first idyllic ramble! It was all very well for Lady Edith to talk about 'our dear changeable Scottish weather,' but the swiftness of the transformation from sunlit Paradise to Wagnerian haunt still amazed her.

There were the usual rustlings and bustlings in the undergrowth, but she guessed they were animal not human. She felt rather happy and, now, not the slightest bit alarmed. After all, compared to her usual solitude, she was surrounded by people, even if most of them were invisible; she was enjoying her birthday—

At which point someone screamed very loudly and sharply just ahead of her on the left. Then there was a splash. Then silence. Jemima ran forward. Somebody else broke cover from behind her. She did not pause to see who it was. After running about fifteen or twenty yards and stumbling slightly, she ran round a corner and slap into Clementina Beauregard who was sobbing and being comforted by Ben. Kim too had come from somewhere. Then Ossian Lucas joined them. Clementina was saying something like this:

'I tell you, I nearly fell in! I was pushed, shoved, I tell you, I nearly went over the bloody cliff! The actual log I was sitting on went in, didn't you hear it?'

'What happened exactly?' Ossian Lucas was breathing heavily but sounded calm as ever.

'I sat down. On a log. I decided to light a cigarette. I began to rummage in my handbag. Flora lay at my feet. The first thing I knew Flora was growling slightly and I knew someone was coming. Then a voice said in a whisper: "Clementina, I name you. You are dead." And then I was shoved, shoved from behind and shoved bloody hard.'

'D'you mean *Dad* shoved you? Why, that's impossible,' said Ben.

'I don't know who shoved me. That's the whole point.'

'I don't believe you were shoved at all,' exclaimed Kim.

'I never said it was Uncle Henry. But someone gave me a push. Whispered and then pushed.'

'You're exaggerating as usual, Clementina,' said Kim scornfully.

'It couldn't possibly have been Dad,' continued Ben in a worried voice. 'He's just named Hamish on the other side of the hill by the cliff. We both spotted Dad and started to stalk him in the bracken. Hamish like an idiot lifted his head and Dad turned round and bagged him. So I skedaddled as fast as I could back through the bracken. Dad did try a long shot after me! "I name you, Rory. You're dead." But as I wasn't Rory, I naturally paid no attention. I've no idea where Rory was. Then I heard Clementina scream. So it couldn't have been Dad.' There was a pause. 'It couldn't have been Dad anyway,' Ben added rather belatedly.

'She's made the whole thing up as usual to get attention.' Kim remained contemptuous. 'I'm getting back on the trail. If Dad was by the cliffs, I'll trail him round the other way, giving the shrine a wide berth . . .'

In the absence of any visible proof of Clementina's ordeal, Jemima had to concede that Kim was probably right. Clementina was in a sufficiently nervous state to have imagined the incident. It was eerie in the mist, near the falls. The high sighing noise made by the rocks did not help matters. When Ben promised to stay close to Clementina for the rest of the stalk, Jemima decided it was time to back away. Perhaps she should retrace her steps; the time of the rendezvous was approaching.

As she reached the gravel path once more, she had the impression that the mist was receding somewhat: at any rate she could see the shape of Tigh Fas distinctly, black and church-like in its outline. In a way she would rather not have glimpsed it at that particular moment, since the familiar feeling of foreboding concerning the house returned more sharply than ever; surely a lady should be feeling joy at the idea of an encounter with her lover, on a romantic Scottish island?

It was more with the idea of galvanizing herself into appropriate feelings of joy, than with any real zest, that she ran up the house steps, through the open door (she must have left it open) and into the hall. There was silence. She heard a movement in the bedroom, then Jacobite came happily tumbling down the stairs, licking her hand gleefully and positively nipping—in a playful manner—at her jean-clad ankles, as though to shepherd her back up the stairs again. Resisting slightly and looking round, her eyes fell on a piece of paper on the hall table; for a moment she thought it was the original note. Then she read: 'I'm upstairs, H.B.B.' He was here!

In her relief, excitement filled her, happiness, and she ran with the dog, up the stairs, and threw open her bedroom door.

'Colonel Henry Beauregard, you are my Prey,' she began to say according to the traditional formula. The phrase was already out of her mouth, the word Prey dying away foolishly, desperately, on her lips, when she realized that the inhabitant of her bedroom was not in fact Colonel Henry.

'On the contrary, Miss Shore, it is you who are my Prey,' said Lady Edith Beauregard in her most pleasant manner. She might have been greeting a guest at Kilbronnack House. But she was standing by the large bed holding a double-barrelled shotgun which was pointing directly and not at all shakily at Jemima's head.

TWENTY

Before You Die

'I'm so glad you managed to come,' continued Lady Edith, the gun unwavering in her hands. 'I've been waiting for this. You see I'm going to shoot you like the other one. Like my sister-in-law Leonie. Isn't it odd,' she said with a fleeting smile, 'that was on my birthday too. But I'd have done it anyway. I'm awfully determined when I set my mind to anything. The maternal instinct, you know. No, of course you don't know, do you? And now you never will.'

The sinister phrase struck a reminiscent note. 'The instinct, being perfected, can go awry. It can be turned towards evil . . .' Mother Agnes's letter, which she could see still lying on her dressing-table where she had left it. Oh, Mother Agnes, you who can see into the human heart. Not Colonel Henry, not Ben, not Rory—but all the time Edith the mother, the centre of it all.

Jemima felt quite frozen, numb. For one thing Lady

Edith continued to talk in her familiar nervous voice, as though apologizing for some fault of whose exact nature she was unaware, while accepting without reservation the fact of her own culpability. The whole situation remained quite unreal. How could Jemima reconcile the fussy, placating personality of Lady Edith with the extraordinary revelations which were now—without hesitation—pouring from her lips?

But even as these revelations were being made, Jemima's mind at least gradually unfroze, and a series of terrible and telling points occurred to her.

Lady Edith babbling on about Leonie Beauregard, horrible, mad:

'She tried to break up the family, you see, so I had to do it, didn't I? Getting hold of my Henry like that.' But then she turned on Jemima: 'And that's why I'm going to kill you too. We're such a happy, happy family, you see. And Henry and I were really the perfect couple, everyone says so. Of course he has to have his little bit of fun from time to time, I do realize that you have to let men enjoy themselves in their own way, which isn't ours, don't you? You know what husbands are . . .'

She paused and gave a little laugh, apologetic as before.

'But how rude of me! You've never been married, have you, Miss Shore? So you don't know what husbands are.' She sounded for one instant quite spiteful, like an unkind child. 'Ladies in London, oh yes, I know all about that. Their letters, sent to the Estate Office, their calls when they think I'm out, their assumed voices when they find I'm in. Silly creatures. I know it all.

'But she was different, Leonie was different. She wanted him to marry her. And so she died. And afterwards we had Kim. That just shows how happy we were really. And you're different too, Miss Shore, and so you will shortly die too.'

'Why am I different?' whispered Jemima. She was ashamed to find that her voice had temporarily deserted her.

'Because you're so tempting, aren't you, Miss Shore? To a man of his age; my Henry isn't young any longer. But you make him feel young, I can see it: he looks more vigorous, he's happier, he laughs, he's even less impatient with me and the boys. Oh, I know, And you're clever and witty and everything he likes, not like those other fools, married women indulging their stupid passions. Why, you're not even married! You're quite, quite free. Father Flanagan pointed it out to me in one of his talks. Oh yes, Miss Shore, you're far too tempting to be allowed to stay in the path of my Henry.

'Besides,' Lady Edith's voice never lost its affability as she spoke; 'besides, you came here. You came to Glen Bronnack. You came into our very own glen, I never allowed any of the others to come here. The Glen belonged to us, to me, and the boys. But you brought it all here, your beauty and your brilliance, you polluted our beloved glen. You came to Eilean Fas on purpose. You wanted to seduce him. You could have had any man in the world, but you chose my Henry. It was all your fault. And I shall kill you here in the house where you did it.'

Jemima felt one single very strong pang of guilt.

Then she reminded herself that there had been other deaths. Ossian Lucas had spoken of the passions that she might stir up, as the waterfall stirred up the dark waters of Sighing Marjorie's Pool. But there had been other deaths before she arrived in the Glen to upset its primitive and precarious balance. Leonie Beauregard, Charles Beauregard...

Nevertheless, that single pang of guilt would remain with her, hidden but ineradicable: it was the voice of Mother Agnes, the voice of her conscience.

She turned her mind, deliberately, as coolly as she could

muster, to investigate the truth of those other deaths. Charles Beauregard, drowned deep in the river, sucked down—what had happened to him, Jemima wondered, in cold appalled amazement. Tremble as she might, she noticed that Lady Edith's grip on the gun remained steady, even vice-like. Jemima made a very slight movement, hardly perceptible, in the direction of the door, still open behind her in the empty house where the mist was now beginning to float lightly in the very air of the interior. At once there was a furious growl, pronounced, minatory, from the dog beside her. She looked down.

'Yes, Jacko, hold her,' said Lady Edith sharply. 'Hold, boy. Now wait.' The dog obeyed her instantly. His teeth closed, without biting or tearing, on Jemima's jeans. He looked up at her, his eyes as soft, as brown, as apparently sympathetic as those of his mistress.

Jacobite. Not Flora but Jacobite. Not Clementina's dog, not Colonel Henry's dog, but Lady Edith's own dog. The well-trained dog; Duncan's words on their first meeting. 'She's wonderful with dogs, her ladyship, trains them herself.'

The details of another death came into her mind. Bridie Stuart, so devoted to Edith Beauregard—who suspected the murderer of Charles but said the truth would never pass her lips . . . What had she seen, what had she known? The dog named by Duncan as Flora, seen near the bridge on the day of Bridie's death, the dog which might have knocked Bridie into the water. How easily that could have been Jacobite! The two dogs were identical, certainly at such a distance.

And Rory, the Chief of the Red Rose, trying to warn Clementina on the telephone. 'You're in danger.' What had he known? Jacobite the bad, Flora the good dog. She had once mistaken the respective characters of Charles and his Uncle Henry Beauregard, making the wrong one good, the wrong one evil. Now she had done the same with the dogs.

She felt she had to know the truth. Jemima Shore, Investigator, might be about to end her days, her pretty telegenic face blown to pieces by a madwoman armed with a shotgun. But she had to know the truth of those deaths.

'The others,' she began, when Lady Edith had finished her fearful disquisition. 'Your nephew Charles, Bridie . . . ?' But Lady Edith was delighted to explain. Her characteristic anxiety, her air of wishing to justify herself, was macabre. She even managed to sound sincerely regretful about Bridie—'I was awfully sorry about that, but you see it just had to be done to protect the family.'

She went on: 'My nephew Charles—well, you could hardly expect me to sit by, could you, while he inherited everything and my own lovely boys got nothing? It was so easy; pretending to Charles that I wanted a rare bog plant growing just above the water line of the pool. I'm famous for collecting wild flowers round here: I knew he'd wade in and get it for me. Charles, in spite of everything,' she said brightly, 'had awfully nice manners. Oh, I knew he'd fall into the trap. We watched. He waded in immediately. And then: so dangerous, those great boots—the times I've warned my boys to take care. We looked after him.'

'We?'

'Jacko and I. Didn't we, Jacko boy? There's a good boy.' The great dog thumped his tail. 'A quick command, in he went, the good dog, swam out, and then so easy to pull a man down in those boots—'

'And Bridie saw you—'

'She saw the dog all wet and coming out of the river as she was bicycling over to Eilean Fas, from the bridge. She didn't know Charles was dead then. She thought it must be Flora. But she found Flora, dry, up at the house, waiting for Charles who never came back. Before she found the body in the river later, Flora followed her down to the river and attacked her. So she knew the first dog must be Jacko. Where Jacko goes, I'm likely to be. And she began to put two and two together. She may even have seen me on the island. I was never sure.'

Jemima thought sadly: But Bridie would never have told what she knew. Lady Edith, after all those years, had not trusted her. How quickly evil—and madness—corrupts the mind.

'So I dashed out of the house on the afternoon of our little royal party, giving as an excuse that I needed Father Flanagan to make the numbers even. And good clever Jacko and I solved the problem of Bridie on that nasty slippery bridge.'

So many clues, thought Jemima. Jacobite—not Flora— seen by Duncan near the bridge on the afternoon of Bridie's death. Lady Edith apparently mismanaging the dinner party so that there was one man over, and actually coolly planning yet another murder to cover her tracks.

'Rory and Hamish did see me training Jacobite, in the woods round Eilean Fas, when they were out pigeon-shooting. But they had their guns with them and were busy arguing about who had just shot what. You know what boys are,' she added indulgently. 'I don't think they suspected anything. Sport means so much to them: why should they bother about what their silly old mother was up to?'

It was not the moment, thought Jemima, to point out that on the contrary both Rory and Hamish had been separately worried—if disbelieving—about what they saw. Rory, in his capacity as Chief of the Red Rose, had imagined that Clementina might be in some kind of danger and had warned her on the telephone. Hamish had paid his inarticulate visit to Jemima somehow trusting that the magic powers endowed by television would enable her to sort out this mute appeal. The trouble was that the brothers had not consulted each other. The suspicion in each case had been too horrible to be given tongue—to another member of the family.

Lady Edith moved a little. The gun now rested on the brass bedrail. Jemima moved too. The dog growled. Jemima stopped moving.

'Time for you to join the stalk, Jacko,' said Lady Edith in an indulgent voice. 'We don't want them to find you here, do we? That would give the game away. Go on, boy, find him, find him.'

Instantly the great golden dog rose and padded out of the room. Jemima could hear him padding down the stairs and out of doors, onto the gravel and away.

'Would you have killed Clementina too?' Jemima put it in the past tense.

Lady Edith smiled warmly. 'I may.' She spoke in the future. 'All that money. After all I've got six hungry boys to provide for. Five, if you don't count Ben, who's provided for now as the eldest. But on the whole, no. Enough is enough. There will have been enough deaths—including yours,' she added. Her tone was wise and compassionate. Jemima was reminded of her first sight of Lady Edith in the church, a face once pretty, blurred by time, the only one showing emotion over the death of Charles Beauregard. Under the circumstances, it was no wonder that she had appeared moved, except that she had been moved by exultation, secret glee, not compassion. But who could ever tell what went on in the crazed murderous mind which lurked beneath the disarming façade of Lady Edith?

'But just now Clementina was pushed. A log fell in. She herself nearly fell in.' Jemima was puzzled. She found it difficult to work out how Lady Edith had managed to get back from the falls in time to greet her.

'Nearly,' repeated Lady Edith with complacency. 'Then that wasn't me at work, was it? I don't make mistakes, do

I? You can't make mistakes when you've got a family to look after. I dare say that naughty Kim was teasing her; he told me he planned to give her a good fright for being so awful to his father in the church. That was why he was so keen on the stalk. I knew I could safely pretend to try and stop it; I could even ask Kim to stay with me for safety's sake. I knew he would never agree. He's such a handful, that boy! Being the baby, I'm afraid he's got a tiny bit spoilt. Still, a miss is as good as a mile, as we used to say in the nursery.'

The silly catch-phrase galvanized Jemima from the strange lethargy into which she had fallen.

'Anyway, Colonel Henry will soon be here to rescue me!' she cried. 'Your husband. I'm expecting him. What are you going to do about that?'

'Oh, please don't bother yourself about Henry,' answered Lady Edith. 'You see I wrote both those little notes to you myself. I don't have your brains, Miss Shore—you couldn't imagine silly old me on television for one moment, could you?—but one thing I can do is imitate Henry's writing quite well after all these years.'

A modest expression of satisfaction crossed her face. 'And I can even imitate your writing too. You wrote me such a sweet note after our little royal party,' said Lady Edith. 'So thoughtful. Such charming manners. It's ridiculous to say people in the press and television are always rude. I shall always remember how good your manners were. "Miss Shore had beautiful manners," I shall say. "Such a pity about her unfortunate death. Trying to handle a gun when she wasn't used to it. We shall never know quite how it happened, or why. We had all grown to love her—Henry, the boys and I. Such a lovely unaffected person."'

Her tone changed abruptly.

'Look, here's the suicide note you've written.' Lady

Edith threw it on the bed with her left hand. Her right hand did not leave the gun's trigger. 'I am sure you'd like to see it. Before you die.'

Jemima leant forward and gingerly took the note from the bed. She read the first few words: 'I can't go on—' She had time to think with the beginnings of panic: 'But they'll never believe this, they won't, Guthrie, Cherry, it's impossible. I'm not like that. I'll tell them. But I won't tell them. It'll be too late, I'll be dead—'

There was a noise behind her on the stairs.

Lady Edith raised the gun. After that, Jemima could never be quite clear about the precise order of events. Lady Edith levelled the gun straight at Jemima. There was a small click—afterwards she realized that was the safety catch being released. Then:

'Edith, don't shoot!' The cry, loud, frantic, almost a bellow, came from directly behind her. It was Colonel Henry's voice. But later the noise of his voice and Lady Edith's own cry: 'No, Henry, not you,' would mingle in her memory with the explosion of the gun, thunderous, enveloping, the force of the explosion which seemed to knock her backwards, sideways. But which in fact turned out to be Colonel Henry knocking her sideways, or possibly rushing in front of her or possibly throwing himself at his wife. She would never know for sure.

All she did know was that when all the noise was over—what seemed to be a million years later, but could only be seconds—she was picking herself up, stunned but physically undamaged, from the bedroom floor. While Colonel Henry continued to lie there. And Lady Edith— with a terrible scream like a tortured animal, a scream she would never forget—had cast down the gun and was running, running down the stairs and away; her footsteps light, fast, sounded on the gravel dying away. Then there was silence. She was gone.

Still Colonel Henry did not move. Delicately, gingerly she touched his black jacket. It was damp. She opened it up. A whole area of the white shirt beneath was stained red, the stain spreading all the time.

'Help, I must get help,' she thought desperately. 'I ought to find someone—but I can't leave him.' She pulled the coverlet off the bed to try and bandage his chest. Then she felt a faint pressure on her fingers. Colonel Henry's hand was on hers. His lips were moving.

'Poor Edith,' he was saying. She could just hear, 'Poor woman.' Jemima continued to staunch desperately at the wound in his chest.

Colonel Henry's lips moved twice more before he stopped moving altogether and lay still. The first time he said something like: 'Till my dying day'—Jemima could not be quite sure, but she hoped he had said that.

Lastly, he said again, 'Poor woman.' Or was it 'Poor women'? She would never know. She only knew that Colonel Henry died as he had lived, a chivalrous man—in either case.

TWENTY-ONE

A Highland Farewell

Much much later Jemima was aware of someone else coming up the stairs with slow steps and then standing over her. She looked up. It was Ossian Lucas.

'Is he dead?' he asked.

Jemima nodded. She had put her little gold mirror to his lips. There was no breath. Then she had closed his eyes gently. She could not bring herself to speak.

'An accident,' said Lucas very firmly, looking at her. 'It was an accident with a gun. You must remember that. We ought to get Father Flanagan and he'll administer the last rites.' Then he said in a softer voice, 'I tried to warn you. I wasn't sure. But I was beginning to suspect. Yet I couldn't believe she would strike again twice in the same way.' There was a pause.

'But to the outside world it was and always will be an accident with a gun.' He repeated in his previous firm tone, 'You must remember that. Close ranks. Protect the family. It's what he would have wanted.'

'Protect the family! Close ranks!' The tears were beginning to pour down her cheeks uncontrollably. 'What about her—' she began. 'It was her, all her—'

'Don't speak,' said Ossian Lucas. 'Not now. Besides, she's gone. Gone for ever. She slipped over the edge of the cliff at the Fair Falls into the pool below. In the fog, you understand. Clementina thought she saw her actually jump over the edge. Absolute nonsense, of course, but Clementina is so excitable; Father Flanagan definitely saw her slip. He tried to save her. It was a tragic accident, like the death of Colonel Henry. That's all.'

'That's all,' repeated Jemima dully after him as if it were a lesson.

She did not stay for his funeral. For after the endless police formalities had been fulfilled and the inquest was over, there was a family funeral.

'What Dad would have liked,' said Ben. No one liked to gainsay Ben now. Besides, he was becoming more authoritarian by the minute. So there would be a piper playing a last lament: a proper Highland farewell.

There was no funeral as yet for Lady Edith because there was no body. The body of the dog Jacobite was discovered floating in Sighing Marjorie's Pool beneath the waterfall. They assumed that the faithful animal had leapt in after his mistress to try and rescue her. But the black depths of the pool refused to give up the body of Lady Edith, and no corpse was ever recovered from the waters into which she had plunged, to forget what she had done, to immerse herself. Later, perhaps, there would be some form of memorial to her in the church of St. Margaret's or a mention of her on Colonel Henry's own gravestone. That too was for Ben to decide.

And Father Flanagan would pray for her, as he prayed

for Colonel Henry, and Leonie, and Charles Beauregard, and all sinners in the eyes of God.

Later still, as Ossian Lucas observed to Jemima Shore, driving her to Inverness to catch the night sleeper, the myths would begin to grow up. Like the bracken at Eilean Fas, they would gradually cover up the neglected truth.

'In another hundred years I dare say it will be called Lady Edith's Pool.'

Jemima thought he was probably right. In another century up the Glen, the legend of the devoted wife and mother, dying to save one of her children, or even her husband, would have succeeded the truth of the jealous, covetous murderess.

Already the deliberate covering-up process had begun. Whatever the police thought privately, it was difficult to shake the combined evidence of the Beauregard family, Father Flanagan the parish priest, and Ossian Lucas the local MP.

'An awful lot of deaths,' said the Kilbronnack constabulary dourly, and later higher police officials echoed the same sentiment. There were enquiries, and doubts, and statements. But in the absence of evidence to the contrary, in the end the verdict was accidental death—on both of them.

After the inquest, Jemima wired Cherry that she was taking the night sleeper south, and wanted to be met (after her experiences which no doubt had been fully reported in the southern press—the family picnic which went wrong and ended in a double tragedy). But she preferred the welcome of a discreet and anonymous chauffeur from Miles and Miles. She made it quite clear in her telegram that the attentions of Guthrie Carlyle would not be well received at that hour in the morning. There would be time for Guthrie—later that day. Or perhaps the next day. Anyway, there would be time for Guthrie in the office, when they were planning the new series, slightly ahead of schedule owing to the abrupt curtailment of her holiday. The trouble with Guthrie was that he was so young. Or did he just seem young to her—now?

She did not want an acolyte. She wanted—she had wanted—she stopped these thoughts. The new series: she would concentrate on that. It was work, not sleep, which had always knitted up the ravelled sleeve of her own particular care.

She received the offer of another set of attentions before she left the Glen. Ben Beauregard paid her a state visit at the Castle, where Jemima had been offered a bed and had accepted a temporary refuge. Ben too seemed a bit young; although Jemima realized afterwards with surprise that they were very nearly the same age.

In a roundabout and graceful manner he attempted to discover whether such attentions would be welcome. Equally gracefully she indicated they would not. At the end of the conversation, Jemima exclaimed impulsively:

'I think you really need someone who would care about land above all else. Or anyway understand the feeling. I could never do that—not feel it, not understand it.' She paused and said in a softer voice, 'In any case, should you not take on Clementina?'

'One way or another, I'll have to take her on,' Ben said musingly. He did not seem put out by Jemima's rebuff. She remembered the scene in the Castle when the girl had taunted him with 'pretty, pretty cousin Clementina.' She thought—in the end—he would take her on. She had once compared Clementina to Rosalind, also a dispossessed heiress. In the end Rosalind had married her Orlando, another victim of a family feud. This Rosalind had found her Orlando. And they would be happy.

She gazed at his handsome, heavy, sombre face so like yet so unlike his father's. At least he would be happy with

Clementina, and with her money, and their castle. Gradually the memory of the past would fade—the memory of his mother, her brother. Clementina would be happy, and have children, a clutch of sons perhaps, the pattern repeating itself—or at least she would be as happy as any woman could be in this man's valley.

Then Ben broke it to her that one woman at least intended to be very happy there.

'Rory and Hurricane Sophie—did you guess? Of course it's a dead secret, more than ever now. As it was, the dreadful snobbish Duchess of Cumberland nearly had a fit when she heard the news and she's the one who controls all the money which will go to Sophie one day from her rich Dutch relations. Roman Catholic! Non-royal! A younger son! They've had to promise to wait till Sophie is twenty-one. And now—well, the only thing to be said is that Sophie is even more obstinate than her mother and for some extraordinary reason she's mad about Rory, so I dare say she'll get her own way in the end.

'I'm going to give them Eilean Fas, by the way. Unbelievably, Rory actually wants to live there, says it's his boyhood dream, and the past makes no difference. The whole of the Highlands is stained with bloody dramas, he said, Eilean Fas no more than anywhere else. Myself,' Ben paused, 'I'd rather die than live there, as you can imagine. But I suppose if anyone can exorcize the ghosts of the Wild Island, it's Hurricane Sophie...'

So Rory had achieved his dream after all. If he could not achieve it one way, he would achieve it another. And he had kept every option open; he had evidently never abandoned his courtship of the spritely Hanoverian princess, while at the same time leading the forces of romantic Stuart reaction on behalf of his secret followers. He had even managed to gratify both parties with the same bold if empty gesture, by making threats against Princess Sophie's personal safety in the name of the Red Rose. The publicity thus generated had been thoroughly welcome on all sides. A very determined if not exactly single-minded man. Or as Bridie Stuart had said long ago, deep.

'Father Flanagan's idea of a mission at Eilean Fas really isn't on—under the circumstances,' Ben added vaguely. 'I've told him I'll do something about it as soon as possible.' But Jemima had a feeling that the day of Father Flanagan's much-desired mission up the Glen would still be long in coming.

At Inverness Station there was another enormous placard in red letters: 'A Highland Farewell to HRH Princess Sophie of Cumberland.' But on this occasion no one, not the Red Rose in mourning, nor some newly formed Black Thistle, had chosen to deface it.

Jemima Shore thought: Unlike Princess Sophie, I won't be coming back to the Highlands. But she was glad that for someone at least Eilean Fas retained, and would always retain, its magic aura of Paradise.

For her the magic was gone. She knew, as she rocketed south in her sleeper, that it was gone, vanished, gone for ever. The very colours of her memories were not the bright clear colours of the Wild Island in sunshine, but other darker shades of regret and loss.

Paradise was not for her. She would not seek it again.

The sleeper swayed and rattled, and the rails beneath the carriage seemed to be carrying out a kind of elaborate quadrille which kept her from falling into unconsciousness, exhausted as she felt. After a while, she put one hand into her handbag to find the ever-present paperback thriller. Her fingers closed unexpectedly on a small cold object. Jemima brought out instead the enamel box which Colonel Henry had given her on the morning of her birthday. She read once more the message held aloft on the lid by two cupids: *Remember Me.*

Yes, she would remember him. Jemima Shore fell asleep still clutching the little box in her hand, so that when she awoke in England, the cold enamel had become warm. But her cheeks were quite wet; she must have been crying in her sleep, a thing which had never happened to her before.

ANTONIA FRASER'S JEMIMA SHORE

Jemima Shore didn't plan on living a life steeped in detection and mystery. But at the age of fifteen, while staying at a Catholic boarding school, she found herself plunged into a bizarre situation involving a suspicious miracle and a flamboyant, manipulative Italian princess.

Now Britain's most popular newswoman, Jemima lives day in and day out with mysteries and danger from every walk of life. That first story, "Jemima Shore's First Case" and all her adventures are now available from Bantam Crime Line Books:

THE MYSTERIOUS WORLD OF AGATHA CHRISTIE

Acknowledged as the world's most popular mystery writer of all time, Dame Agatha Christie's books have thrilled millions of readers for generations. With her care and attention to characters, the intriguing situations and the breathtaking final deduction, it's no wonder that Agatha Christie is the world's best-selling mystery writer.

☐ 25678	**SLEEPING MURDER**	$3.95
☐ 26795	**A HOLIDAY FOR MURDER**	$3.50
☐ 27001	**POIROT INVESTIGATES**	$3.50
☐ 26477	**THE SECRET ADVERSARY**	$3.50
☐ 26138	**DEATH ON THE NILE**	$3.50
☐ 26587	**THE MYSTERIOUS AFFAIR AT STYLES**	$3.50
☐ 25493	**THE POSTERN OF FATE**	$3.50
☐ 26896	**THE SEVEN DIALS MYSTERY**	$3.50

Buy them at your local bookstore or use this page to order.

BANTAM MYSTERY COLLECTION